My Brother
Stealing Second

My Brother
Stealing Second

Jim Naughton

HARPER & ROW, PUBLISHERS, New York
Grand Rapids, Philadelphia, St. Louis, San Francisco,
London, Singapore, Sydney, Tokyo

Library of Congress Cataloging-in-Publication Data
Naughton, Jim.
   My brother stealing second / Jim Naughton.
      p.   cm.

   Summary: After his older brother is killed in a car accident, sixteen-year-old Bobby tries
to come to terms with some disturbing truths about his family and political corruption in
their town as well as deal with his profound grief and the beginnings of first love.
   ISBN 0-06-024374-0 : $
   ISBN 0-06-024375-9 (lib. bdg.) : $
   [1. Brothers—Fiction.   2. Grief—Fiction.   Death—Fiction.
4. Family problems—Fiction.]   I. Title.
PZ7.N17477My   1989   88-22035
[Fic]—dc19   CIP
                                                                              AC

For my parents, Frank and Alice Naughton,
with love and gratitude

My Brother
Stealing Second

1

We live in Reese Point now, on a crescent-shaped street with a wooded hillside across the way. Hollow Hill Road isn't the fastest route to anywhere, so there's never much traffic. Sometimes I think that's why my father chose this place. We are hidden, but he doesn't have to admit to himself that we are in hiding. Personally, I'd like to live on Main Street and make *them* deal with us.

The first thing I hear most mornings is the brawling between Mrs. Williver's raggedy old cats and the blue jays that nest on the hillside. The jays can't win—whoever heard of a bird eating a cat?—but they attack like kamikazes just the same, swooping in, eyeball high. Cats don't have the nerve for that kind of thing, so they end up hightailing it back beneath the porch. I root for the birds.

My father is just out of the shower, padding around in his socks and underwear. Of all the things that have changed in the last seven months, nothing eats at me like the sight of Dad in colored socks. They make his legs look skinny and pale, but you pretty much have to wear them with a shirt and tie.

Everybody says my father looks great now that he's out of the ash works and into the office, but I don't know. His shape seems completely unfamiliar to me. Dad has been swallowed by his sports coat. At least he still wears the Polywaxen County A. C. windbreaker we gave him. And his Pirates hat. My father thinks he is still part of the Pittsburgh Pirates' organization the way some of his buddies from Korea think they are still part of the Army.

Downstairs my mother is fixing breakfast. I eat breakfast mostly because Mom likes to make it, and because I let her down in so many other ways. She thinks eating breakfast together is a sign of our progress as a family. That's a pretty hot topic around here: *our progress as a family.* It's like we are in an experiment, or maybe a zoo, and that even while we are hiding, somebody is watching us. *"This week on* Wild Kingdom, *Jim and I visit the Connelys, a reclusive Pennsylvania tribe."* Sometimes I think I screw up for the audience's sake, so they won't get bored and I won't lose their attention.

Until eight o'clock each morning I lie in bed, staring at posters of Lou Gehrig and Humphrey Bogart. When the whistle blows at the ash works, I roll out of bed and take my shower. It is not that I don't like getting up. Mom's coffee smells great in the kitchen. The sun and the bare trees throw cool-looking shadows on the hillside across the street. But I've been at the table when the whistle blows and watched my parents go stiff. It takes a long time

4

for the conversation to get going again. Sometimes I wonder if each of them hates the other, right then, for not having anything graceful to say.

The weird thing is that in about five minutes, they are back to normal. That's what pisses me off. It's like: *A quick shot of grief each morning leaves me free for the rest of the day.* As though it's an antiperspirant or something.

That's not my style. I like to wallow in my grief. I make a cloak out of it and wrap it around myself. I take it up on the roof on windy nights, and believe it will help me fly. When the Ash—which is all we call it—works overtime, the whistle for the last shift blows at two A.M. and I never fall asleep before I hear it.

I read until late—novels mostly, with characters my own age, to see which of us is more messed up. When I get tired, I think about my brother. This is the best time for remembering him because I'm too exhausted to go crazy. I just drift from one memory to another on my way down to sleep. It's like being a scuba diver, swimming through this great world you can't ever live in.

Here's my favorite dive—My brother stealing second: off and back, real nonchalantly, smirking at the pitcher like, Why bother? Off and back again, but this time the play is close and he jams his foot into the base just ahead of the tag.

The pitcher is thinking, I don't know what the big deal is with this guy. I can get him with my good move. Which is just what Billy wants him to think. When the guy spins and cuts loose, my brother tosses himself chest first into the dirt. His right hand hits the bag before the first baseman can take a swipe at him.

5

"Safe," the umpire says.

He was always safe. He was always smiling, too, though just barely, as he dusted himself off, because now he knew what he needed to know. Billy kept a book on the pick-off moves of every pitcher in our league, and he passed it on to me. Jackie Hochreiter angles his left foot toward third. Brian Kuchar cocks his right hip toward first. Reg Moody pauses a beat longer at the belt if he is going to the plate. Tony Moran triple-checks the runner.

By his junior year Billy could steal on anybody in our corner of the state. I'd seen him get such a big jump that catchers would stand up and shrug their shoulders. Those weren't my favorite times, though. Once against Brewerton they pitched out when Billy was running. The throw had him beat, but he dove in on his stomach, swung his body in toward the mound, and sneaked a hand in as he slid by the bag. We had a little signal between us, kind of a long distance high-five. Billy would stand up and clap his right hand to his left elbow. That day he looked me right in the eye when he did it.

Anyway.

Aside from the whistle, my mother and father are pretty chatty at breakfast. We are very big on "activities" at our house. My parents are always talking about the Block Association, the Holy Name and the Altar and Rosary societies. But I get the feeling they don't really participate in these meetings. I think they just go and sit in the back of the room.

The trouble with not doing very much is that you discuss everything you *do* do in ridiculous detail. If we are driving to Lake Epinesset on Saturday, my mother asks us what kind of sandwiches we want by Wednesday. That's about the time when Dad finishes kicking around Father Streeter's sermon on what Jesus meant when he said the truth would set you free. Or whatever it was that Jesus said that week.

It wasn't so bad before my parents went on their self-help book binge. But I must admit I've picked up some pretty spiffy phrases from listening to their conversations. I even know what the school psychologist is talking about when he tells people I've been "acting out." I've heard all the techniques about becoming my own best friend and I can recite the seven stages of grief from memory. Backward. Maybe that beats small talk, but it sits pretty heavily with a plate of scrambled eggs.

My mother drops me at school on her way to the Valley Vista Sears where she sells shoes. Most mornings she says I look tired and threatens me with "a good thorough checkup." Sometimes she wants to know why I never bring any of my friends home. When she's really reaching, she'll ask if I've given any thought to going out for baseball.

I say no, which is not exactly a lie. I think about baseball all the time, but I don't think about playing for Reese Point. Reese Point baseball is a joke. We beat them so badly last season that Coach Sherrill put me and the other freshmen in for three innings, just to hold the score down. No one who played for the Ryder Wildcats would *ever* play for Reese Point, even if he *was* forced to go to school there. That's the one piece of pride I don't have to swallow each morning before I walk into that building.

For the most part I deal with school by pretending I'm

7

not there. As a result, I'm doing great in all but one of my classes. The teacher's voice is like the Walkman they give you at the dentist's office. The noise helps take your mind off all the brutal stuff that's happening to you.

My only problem is in social studies where we break into groups and talk about "issues." I'm more or less opposed to class participation. The welt under my left eye is from the day I started a fight with Eddie Ciccone. He knows nothing whatsoever about alcoholism.

In his office that day Mr. Ianetta said: "I know this is hard for you Bobby, but you've got to try to get along here. You and your parents are part of our community."

But it isn't true. My parents and I are on a boat no harbor will have, and actually, I am not even sure we are on the same boat.

2

In social studies we are reading about the new immigrants. The teacher is a sub in a green dress whose name I forget. She is taking the class for the whole week. Mrs. Greendress thinks it might help us understand the subject a little better if we write a paper about how our families came to live where we live. She is talking about famines and revolutions, but I can feel everybody's eyes on me. This is an unlucky class. Mr. Kerrins is a jerk, but he never would have let this happen.

Annie Dunham doesn't look at me. She never does. But I figure she's got to be freaking out, too. For a while I stare at the side of her face and then past her out the window.

"Mr. Connely," Greendress says, scaring the hell out of me.

"Ma'am?"

"I'd like you to read yours to the class."

9

"When's that, ma'am?"

"At the end of the period."

I hear some people whispering. Kids are shifting in their seats like they're the ones with something to be uncomfortable about. Annie Dunham folds her hands in front of her face and tucks her thumbs under her chin like she's saying a prayer. The sub reads her name, too. This can't happen.

I can't remember Greendress's name, so I keep calling her "Ma'am?"

"Yes, Mr. Connely?"

"I'm afraid I won't be able to do this, ma'am."

"And why not?"

I try to go up and tell her, but she says, "I think the class can share this."

I sink back down, trying to think up a good quick lie, but nothing comes to me.

"Mr. Connely!" She is yelling, but I don't really hear her because I'm on my way out the door.

She doesn't follow me, not right away, and by the time she does, I'm down the stairs milling with the kids who have fourth period lunch. I see her pounding down the hallway, straight for Strank's office. He's the dean of discipline. But once he hears my name, he'll just refer her to Ianetta, the school shrink.

Sometimes I think my role in life is to keep Mr. Ianetta humble. He's got a hold on everybody else's problems, all the underachievers and the kids from broken homes, but he doesn't have a clue with me.

I cut out the back door and jog onto the football field

where Mr. Czarneki has a gym class. Some kid kicks a soccer ball too far and I chase it into the woods, roll it back out, and wait to see if anybody notices I'm gone. Nobody does.

Once I make the woods, I run down to the river and follow the water all the way to Reese Point Rag. It's nearly noon, so I wait by the gate for the day shift to file into the Barefoot and drink lunch. The guy I'm looking for is Cowboy Charley.

Cowboy Charley's name is McCrimmon. He's twenty-three, really smart, and laconic as hell. The only reason I know what laconic means is that I heard some guy describe Charley that way and looked it up.

The Cowboy dropped out of college a couple of years ago, but that's still one of the only subjects he'll say much about. He reads a lot of philosophical books and smokes a ton of pot. When I worked at Rag last summer he let me hang around with him. They called us Mac 1 and Mac 2. As it turns out, he is already in the Barefoot.

"Before Christ." He calls me that because of my initials.

"Hi, Charley."

"What's the rub?"

"School sucks."

"Don't it? When I was at Bucknell . . ." Most times when I mention school to Charley he gets into "When I was at Bucknell." He's got a lot of old-man-type stories for such a young guy. Sometimes I never even get around to telling him what's happened. He just goes on and on, then asks me if I'm getting laid, or if I ever had an out-of-body experience or something like that.

11

". . . so this prof is trying to tell me there's no connection between Percy and Kierkegaard. Hadn't even read the damn literature."

"Can you skate?"

"Can Gretzky?"

"Let's skate then."

Skating is what the Cowboy calls taking the afternoon off. We did it about once every other week when I worked at the Rag. All it took was a couple of six-packs and a little dope.

Charley pushes his cycle out past the plant where no one can hear the engine roar, and we follow the old river trail up above Ryder. The water is still clean in the mountains, so you can go diving off the Stones and swim inside the caves.

The Stones are about forty feet high and Charley is the most daring guy who ever set foot on them, especially when he is high. One day a kid broke his spine when he dove too far trying a flip from the Big Chair. You could hear the bones cracking all the way down that part of the canyon. The next day, when the police lines came down, Charley climbed the Chair and flipped, just to prove it could be done.

We build a fire, split a sandwich from Lucy's, and drink most of the beer. Charley has a blanket in his pack, so after we smoke a little pot, I wrap it around myself and fall asleep against a rock. When I wake up, it's just about dark. Charley is standing over me, drying himself with a towel. His skin is blue, but he's not shivering.

"BC," he says, "you're too young to live like a refugee."

"I have that album," I say.

"Serious. What's the shake-up today?"

When I tell him about school he is quiet for a long time. "Why didn't you do it?" he asks finally.

"Right."

"Serious, BC."

"Too many people know about it already," I say. "Their daughter is in that class, too, you know. It would have been pretty brutal on her."

"Reading it would have sucked," he says. "But writing it down, man. When I was at Bucknell, we had this one prof . . . the hell with Bucknell. I'm just saying, writing it down can be pretty decent. It's like making up your own self-help book."

I think of all those paperbacks in our magazine stand.

"Yeah, I'll call it *I'm a Jerk, You're a Jerk,*" I say.

The Cowboy drops me on the other side of town and I zigzag through the village so nobody will know where I'm coming from. I know I am incredibly spaced out, because I walk straight down Willow Street, which is where Annie Dunham's aunt and uncle live. It is also where Annie Dunham lives now. And she is stepping down from her bus when I turn the corner. It makes me wish I could disappear.

I say hello, because how could you not? She says hello, too. For a couple of seconds we just stand there, not really looking at each other. Then she says, "Thank you."

By the time I manage to ask "For what?" she is already halfway down the block.

We usually eat dinner at five thirty, but it is just about

13

six when I walk into the kitchen. My parents are sitting at the table, looking at their folded hands. I've been missing about six hours.

"Bobby," they say and stand up fast. But all of the rest of it gets bitten off. This is kid gloves time and they are waiting to see what I'll do.

"Don't be mad," I say. "I just went for a walk. I just needed to go for a walk."

Climbing the stairs, I try to show them as much cool as I can. Two summers ago Billy swiped a Do Not Disturb sign from the Bayberry Inn in Wildwood, New Jersey, so I hang that on the door. This is the beginning of when I went to sleep for a week.

Diving

We are sitting on a wall at Iroquois Park. Me and Billy and my cousin Joey beside a huge statue of Humpty Dumpty. Uncle Jimmy and my dad have gone for popcorn, but Aunt Gracie is there, smiling her big pink-lipstick-on-the-teeth smile. Mom fiddles with the camera. I'm about four at this point. Billy is six. Joey is two.

"One more time," Aunt Gracie says. "Say 'Cheeeese-burgers.' "

"Cheese boogers," Billy says.

Mom snaps the picture and Dad calls her to help him with the sodas. Aunt Gracie comes to take us off the wall. "You two first," she says to Billy and Joey, who sit on the egg's left. "A big boy in this arm and a bigger boy in this one."

"I'm jumping down," Billy says.

The wall is about four feet high.

"Me too," I say.

"Well I guess that leaves you for me," Aunt Gracie tells Joey. "Here comes the airplane in for a landing." She tickles his ribs and lifts him into the air.

"It's pretty far," Billy says when she's gone. "Here goes."

Pushing off with his hands and his rear, he drops to the ground and falls over frontward. I figure he'll start crying because I know I would have. But he just stares at me like it is my fault for watching. Then he runs off.

I sit still. Getting tickled in the ribs and thrown up in the air doesn't seem like that bad a deal. "Here comes the airplane in for a landing." But nobody notices I'm missing. "Mom," I yell. "Mommy." But she doesn't hear me.

No one hears me until Billy catches up with them and shows off his bruises. Uncle Jimmy comes to the wall because Mom is looking at Billy's knees and Dad has his hands full of soda.

3

I take a shower and close the bedroom door. Without drying off, I step into gym shorts and open up the window. It gets pretty cold pretty fast, but I just stand there shivering. After a while, when my hair begins to freeze, I hang my head out the window and pretend I am one of those icy trees you see along Route 81 after a winter rain.

This is a damn good way to catch cold, which is exactly what I am trying to do. Sometimes I think I am the happiest when I have a cold. I *know* my father is the happiest when I have a cold, because it is the only time he knows what to do for me. It's like being sick makes me approachable.

For some reason I think my mother is onto me, so I sniffle and hack a lot when she comes in before work. I even rub my cold nose against her wrist when she puts her hand on my forehead. This makes me feel like a spaniel, but what the hell, it does the trick.

When the house is empty, I drop about four Contac and catch a deep nod. I spent about six hours one day running my eyes over this sunspot that was moving across the rug toward my bed. I pretended it was a camp, with animals and wagons and campfires, like the Israelites running away from Pharaoh's army. I bet the guys who wrote *Star Trek* were on antihistamines the whole time.

Usually I can catch exactly as much cold as I need to get a few days off without anybody wondering if there is something seriously wrong with me. But the night after I went to the river with Charley, I must have overdone it because I was knocked out for the better part of four days. Not that I noticed the time passing, but when I woke up on Friday I saw that my mother had covered me with her quilt. That's about as close as anybody in our corner of the state comes to practicing witchcraft.

The quilt isn't just a blanket, it's a history lesson. Mom started sewing it when she was seventeen, and every piece of material stands for an important event in her life. There's a swatch of her green high school uniform stitched into the maroon bib of her cheerleading outfit. A shiny patch of prom-dress blue borders the scratchy gray vest from Dad's tux.

Everybody wears green in the Army, so she's got some of that in there. It is joined to the gray-and-white flannels Dad wore on the Pirates farm teams. Those are stitched into Mom's Woolworth smock, which borders the plaid vest she wore to give out the gifts for S&H Green Stamps.

All this happened before they were married. I'm sure

about the timing because right below my chest the black silky stripe from his pants is sewn into her bridal veil.

The rest of my body was covered with scraps of clothing that my brother and I had worn. There were flimsy white gowns for baptism and dark-blue ties for First Communion. Confirmation is the only time in my life I've ever worn red and it wasn't voluntarily. Mom even stitched in some black silk from the shorts I wore as a page in the May Crowning, easily the most embarrassing event of my life. Good thing the Church has so many ceremonies for kids, though, or my feet would have stuck out.

I can see where Billy turned nine because the quilt is almost all uniforms after that. Our Little League and Biddy Basketball jerseys are all mixed up in Dad's softball pants and bowling shirts.

When we were kids, Billy and I couldn't tell how sick we were until Mom decided what blankets to give us. She had this ratty blue one for colds and a couple of prickly brown things for the flu. Lying beneath the quilt, though, was a whole 'nother story. She saved that for strep throat, chicken pox, and measles, both German and domestic. When I was a kid I used to think it healed me.

Mom didn't really have a design for the quilt. She just sewed pieces on when she was in the mood. It looked like an amoeba with frayed edges. "Why don't you put a border on it?" I asked her once. "Because it isn't finished," she said.

I was thinking about that when I felt something smooth on my cheek. It was a deep purple material, and although I can't say for sure I'd bet it was from a pall, like the ones they put over caskets at funerals. Like I said, I can't say for sure. I took a pass on the funeral. They may have draped the damn coffin in his old Michelob beach towel for all I know.

I didn't much care what the pall stood for in church, but what it stood for on the quilt scared the shit out of me. All of a sudden I sat up, pushed it off, and kicked it onto the floor.

The border on the quilt was like Mom's suicide note. I freaked out about that until I started freaking out about why she'd sent it to *me*. Ever since Billy died people have sort of shielded me from their grief. I think they are afraid of what I might do.

Which I probably would have done, if I could have figured out how to do it. We don't keep any guns in our house, or the right kind of pills. I'm not a jumper like Charley and razor blades give me the creeps—although I do know that if you're going to slit, you slit vertical. I wouldn't mind if I ceased to exist, but I'd just as soon skip killing myself. Once I stuck my head in a plastic bag for twenty minutes and all I got was a rash on my neck.

My mother would know how to do it, though. She could do it in a minute. The more I thought about that, the more I thought that I shouldn't be around to see what it would look like.

Maybe jumping wouldn't be that tough. I crossed the room and heaved up the window. Sitting on the sill, I rubbed my eyes fiercely enough to grind them through the back of my head. It wouldn't be that hard to tip backward and land on your neck. At least you'd get crippled. At least they wouldn't care if you stopped trying so hard.

I think I might have done it except I began to imagine

people standing around my body down at Knight's saying what a tragedy it was. Except that wasn't what they'd be saying. They'd be saying that I followed Billy dead, just like I followed him alive. It wouldn't even be my death, just the rest of his. I hated him for that. I hated him for leaving and not leaving me an escape. Even the Big Escape looked like some kind of tribute to him.

I guess that's when it hit me that I was stuck. Stuck with him, stuck with me, stuck with what had happened and what everybody knew about it. Thing was, I wasn't really sure what I knew about it myself.

Charley said that maybe I could learn something from *writing it down, man.* I closed the window and found a bunch of loose-leaf paper in my desk drawer. That is when I started this. I thought I would just tell about my brother and how he died, but I kept going back and back.

4

We were heading cross-county in the station wagon to see the Pirates' Double A team play in Darden. I think I was eight, although I could have been ten, because all those summers seemed the same. My father merged into traffic and I sat in the back announcing the trip, play-by-play style, like the sportscasters on TV.

"Chris, Wild Bill Connely has just passed another car. I think it's a Buick. That's his fifth pass since he's swung onto Route 81. This young driver is really going places. Here he comes up on an Oldsmobile and *swoosh*, right past. Next in sight is a U-Haul. Should be a piece of cake for the gentleman from Ryder, Pa. Now back to you in the booth."

I didn't realize it at the time, but my father was actually racing backward. He'd spent six years in the minor leagues for Pittsburgh after he was discharged from the service.

First he played centerfield, then right, and finally left. One day, after his second season of Triple A ball, they told him his career was over. Just like that.

According to Mom, he was broke at the time and I don't guess he had any skills other than stealing signs and hitting behind the runner. He must have felt like the best part of his life was over when he came home to ask his old friend Cy Ryder for a job at the Ash.

The Ryders have run the Ash for three generations. Without it there wouldn't be much reason for Ryder to exist. Reese Point, either. You're always reading in the papers about what great civic boosters they are and how they've rejected a slew of buy-out offers to keep their headquarters here. People are so thrilled about it that they'll give them just about anything they ask for. Cy Ryder's brother, Bernie, asked to be sheriff. His brother-in-law, Mr. Silber, asked to be the DA's right-hand guy. Every now and then Cy asks for more land in Reese Point to build another waste bed.

Everybody knows how much they owe the Ryders, but everybody kind of wishes they didn't. That's why my dad was more than just another guy in the shop when he came home. He was the one who was supposed to get away. My mom has an old scrapbook of Dad's clippings from our local papers. They make him sound like Joe DiMaggio. Or at least Dom DiMaggio. People must have figured that if Dad couldn't beat the Ash, nobody around here could.

So we'd be in the car, either speeding to Darden or speeding to the Little League. We were always speeding and it was always baseball. Billy must have seemed like a first-class blessing the day my father figured out that if he wasn't exactly a natural, then he was nearly one. My brother in the hole for a grounder. My brother leaping a runner to turn a double play. My brother smashing an opposite-field double. My brother stealing second.

Stealing second was the heart of it, because even though he was gifted, he wasn't very big. Billy was only five foot eight when he died and Mom didn't think he'd get much taller. He never weighed more than 134 pounds. He was just fast and graceful, and he knew baseball like he'd been living with it for a thousand years.

I remember a graduation, or maybe it was a christening, when I overheard one of my mother's aunts say, "None of the Connely men were ever very *big*, were they?" Which I took to mean that we weren't really men at all. I guess that is why when I watched Billy slide in in front of a tag I felt glad for about four generations of Connely men, who were never really very *big*, were they?

In Billy's junior year, Ryder won the Tri-County championship. He was the all-league shortstop. Richie Munley was the all-league centerfielder. Mark Ryder, Cy's son, made second team all-state as a left-handed pitcher. At the end of the season all three of them got scholarships to Blackie Sherwood's baseball clinic at Darden State. *Going* to the clinic was no big deal. Lots of rich kids who couldn't play worth a damn got their parents to pay for it. But getting one of Blackie's scholarships usually meant that he wanted you for DSU's team and that meant you might get a scholarship there.

That part of it didn't matter much to Mark—his dad had already put three kids through Villanova. But for Richie and my brother it was their best shot at making it to college. Anyway, the word we got was that Billy played his ass off that week. People said he impressed the hell out of everybody and had at least one scholarship offer more or less in the bag. Of course maybe they only said so later, to make us feel better.

The other big deal about Blackie's camp is the final night party. All these seventeen- and eighteen-year-old kids invade East Marine, a little lake town about halfway between here and Darden. In the process of hopping from one bar to another they get shitfaced, chase older women, et cetera. My brother, as it happened, could do that with the best of them, which he was.

At two A.M. that night he, Richie, and Mark, along with all the other party boys from Blackie's camp, were asked to leave Joltin' Joe's Juke Joint. Joe's is more or less a redneck place where the men are called Pointers and the women are called Setters on the rest-room doors.

At roughly two fifteen, in the resort area of Tamble Ridge, their car rounded a thirty-five-mile-an-hour curve at nearly sixty-five miles an hour and collided head-on with another. The passengers in that car were a husband and wife celebrating their eighteenth wedding anniversary.

Mark Ryder crawled out of the wreck uninjured. Richie Munley was pulled from the backseat with a broken right leg and a busted kneecap.

My brother died.

So did Annie Dunham's mom and dad.

This is harder than I thought.

The sheriff's investigation showed that the vehicle at fault was Mark's Mustang and that the driver of that vehicle was William P. Connely, Jr. But they didn't announce any of that stuff until after the funerals. After the funerals was when everything started to change, but nothing happened the way I thought it would.

I figured Annie Dunham's family would sue us, but that didn't happen. I thought my father might lose his job, but Cy Ryder made him a clerk instead. The only thing I guessed right about was moving out of town. I don't know if Cy Ryder thought that up, or if it really was Dad's idea. "We don't need all the room" was his official explanation, but come on.

Reese Point is just west of Ryder, but the two towns are separated by a small hill. It is possible to live in one place and almost never have anything to do with the other. Most of us like it that way. The people in Ryder think they are better than we are, but really they just live in a better place.

Most of it has to do with the Ash. The wind usually carries the soot in our direction and all the leftover gunk gets poured into waste beds on Boulevard Avenue. Actually, half our town is built on waste beds.

Sludge from the Ash still gets pumped into underground tunnels in Reese Point, even though the government is making them stop that. And some kind of chemicals have poisoned our part of the river. People in Ryder think of this as their dumping ground and I guess they are probably right.

My dad picked out the house here and, like I said, it's a great hiding place. But he didn't notice all the details like where Annie Dunham's aunt and uncle live.

I quit writing and push my chair back from the desk.

The quilt is still lying on the floor. I stare at it for a little while and gradually figure out what happened. It wasn't my mother who took it out of the cedar chest. It was my dad.

Just that second the door opens. Mom's eyes go straight to the quilt. She looks at it like it's Billy's ghost. "I never meant for you to see that," she says.

"I know."

She crouches beside my chair. "It was just something I did at the time," she says.

"I hope that's all you do."

It took her a second to figure out what I meant. "Oh, sweetheart, I never would."

"Me either," I say. And it feels like I mean it.

Diving

Phil Larkin has a glass eye. My mom said he wasn't much of a barber, but my dad liked to go to him because they went through school together. Dad used to help Phil find his eye when it got knocked out during high school football games.

Once, when it was time for haircuts, Mom and I were in town at the dentist. "I thought we'd get your hair cut while we were out," she said. I knew I was screwed then, because Phil's Place was only two blocks from the house.

She took me to some guy named Mr. Anthony. Phil had pictures of ballplayers on his walls, but this guy had pictures of hairstyles. "We'll augment the natural wave," he said.

I looked at Mom like he'd suggested peeling my eyeballs.

"That sounds fine," she said.

It wasn't fine. The front of my hair came out looking like the swoosh on a pair of Nikes. To make things worse he put *hair spray* on it. I wished it was winter so I could squash it down with a skully or else Friday so I wouldn't have to go to school.

When we got home, Billy was sitting there with his normal haircut. "You got scalped royal," he said.

Dad looked me over, but he didn't say anything. "You get yours cut too?" he asked Mom.

"No," she said.

"I thought I smelled hair spray." He looked at me again and realized what had happened. I could tell he felt sorry for me. Billy didn't.

"You got hair spray? You did. You got *hair spray* like a girl. You went to the hairdresser."

"I did not."

"Bobby went to the beauty parlor. Bobby went to the beauty parlor."

When I took a bath that night I rubbed about half a bar of soap on my hair. It didn't feel so funny after that, but it still looked the same. Billy told his friends about it too, so school was pretty brutal.

5

Sunday night we blew a fuse. My father fixed it right away, but nobody remembered to turn our clocks ahead. The next morning, at what I thought was 7:41, I woke up screaming.

Most days I get ready for the whistle the way a quarterback gets ready to be sacked. But that morning the whistle blindsided me. I was still in bed, lying on my stomach, trying to focus my eyes on Gehrig when it blew.

This huge fist shot up out of the mattress straight into my chest and plowed me backward. When Dad came in, I was kneeling on the bed at the tail end of hyperventilating. My heart was beating in my eardrums. The chills went away, but my hands kept shaking.

"Are you okay?" my dad said.

I nodded, without looking at him. I wished he'd leave, and after a while he did.

At first I was going to grab the clock radio and smash it off the wall, but instead I just picked it up and tried to reset the minute hand. By the time I managed to get 8:04, the deejay said it was 8:06. My hands kept shaking, so when I hit 8:07, it had to have been 8:08, and so on.

Sometimes when I'm losing it like that I talk to myself. I pretend I'm two people, but it's like they don't really know each other. One guy is trying to make friends, but the other guy won't let him because he thinks nobody can understand him. The friendly guy never wins.

"My brother is dead."

"I'm sorry."

"You're sorry, but you don't understand."

"I *do* understand."

"Maybe you understand, but you can't *know.*"

"You're right, I can't know."

"Who could know?"

"Annie Dunham said, 'Thank you.'"

"*Annie* Dunham. She must see her parents dead every time she looks at me."

"And when you look at her?"

"That's different. It was His Fault."

"Not yours."

I don't think I heard a word anybody said to me that day, a net loss of about three sentences. All morning I kept thinking up opening lines. "Hi, how are you?" is usually pretty decent, but it doesn't exactly flow into "So, my brother killed your folks and I was wondering if you felt like talking about it."

Mr. Kerrins was back in social studies Monday. We

were discussing Ethiopians. Everybody was opposed to mass starvation, and that made me so proud of them that I almost started walking around the room, shaking hands.

"Congratulations, Eddie, you compassionate little bugger. I never would have expected this from you. You're such a jerk most of the time."

I was wondering if he would have taken another swing at me when Annie Dunham started to say something about "the political aspect of the problem." Hearing her voice again reminded me of last Friday on Willow Street.

The Cowboy says all of our senses have memories, so I must have been in audio mode just then. I heard her say "Thank you," over and over again. I still didn't know what she meant. *Ask about that.*

"Bobby Connely," Mr. Kerrins said. "What do you think about that?"

I was caught dead.

"Uh, I agree with Annie. Miss Dunham," I said and felt my face get hot.

"Which part?"

"Oh, the whole thing. I thought it was an astute analysis."

"Anything to add?"

"No. She pretty much summed it up."

"Nice try. See me after class."

"Although I myself do feel that the crisis, ah, may be of such magnitude that, um, perhaps the Ethiopian government should consent to the, ah, intervention of an international body to, like, aid in establishing settlement patterns for the refugees."

I'd read that on the Op-Ed page of the *Inquirer* that

weekend. I didn't exactly know what it meant, but I went for it. It was better than losing track of Annie Dunham.

"After class," Kerrins said again.

"With an eye toward the reestablishment of indigenous cultures. I mean customs."

"After class."

"I can't," I said. "Doctor's appointment," which was a lie.

"He's getting his head shrunk," Eddie Ciccone said.

I started to spin around in my seat, but then stopped. I hate it when I let that asshole know he gets to me.

"Eddie!" Kerrins said.

"There's not going to be anything left to it," Eddie said.

"That would make us just about even," I said.

"Class dismissed," Kerrins said. "Except for you two."

After everybody left, Kerrins buzzed the office on the intercom. "Tell Mr. Ianetta I'm sending Bobby Connely up," he said sounding wearier than he had a right to.

The school psychologist, who is *not* technically a shrink, is wedged into this tiny office between the chemistry and bio labs on the top floor. Going to see him makes you feel like an exile or an afterthought. *Here's where we hide our problems.* The office is spartan as hell: cinderblock walls, linoleum floor, black metal desk, three uncomfortable chairs, and a wire table buried beneath copies of *Psychology Today.*

Ianetta is a stocky guy with a blond mustache who loves velour. Not at all like the reedy-looking shrinks with those half glasses that I'd seen right after Billy died.

"Hello, Bobby," he said, without getting up. "I haven't seen you in what, two weeks? Real progress."

33

"Well, I was sick for one of those, so I don't think it counts."

He looked genuinely disappointed. "What's the latest escapade?"

He always calls my problems escapades, which sort of makes them sound like something that happened to Bob Hope and Bing Crosby. Bobby Connely starring in *The Road to Nowhere.*

"I think Mr. Kerrins thinks I'm upset because somebody in his class said something stupid to me."

"And are you?"

"Not exactly. Not a lot."

"Was it Eddie Ciccone?"

I nodded.

"Have you been having trouble with any of your other classmates?"

"Not that I know of."

"Making any friends?"

"Not that I know of."

"Do you think you're any closer to that?"

When I don't feel like talking I stare at my sneakers. But not even a pair of high white Converses is reassuring all the time. I still wanted to talk to Annie Dunham, but she'd probably left for the day.

I'm not usually that straight with Ianetta because I don't want him knowing too much. But he was trying to help me, which is more than I could say for anybody else around that place. I felt like I should tell him something. So I said, "A little bit." Whispered it more like, at the tips of my sneakers. "Maybe I need somebody to talk to."

"That's very important," he said. "I'd like to explore that with you . . ."

I started shaking my head.

". . . but I'm afraid we can't do it right now. I've got another appointment. We'll make another time."

I nodded at him, or maybe I just meant to. It was weird for Ianetta to hustle me out of the office like that, especially after I'd actually told him something. I was sinking into a funk and wouldn't have noticed his next appointment sitting on the floor in the hallway if I hadn't just about tripped over her.

Annie Dunham. She was wearing gray hiking boots that I almost stepped on, gray jeans, and a deep-blue sweater. Her hair, her eyes, and the freckles on her cheeks are all exactly the same shade of brown, chestnut, I think. She was pretty beautiful, but I remember that now more than I noticed it then.

"I'm sorry," she said when I quit the balancing act.

"No, it was my fault."

She stood up, holding her books in one arm and brushing off the seat of her pants with the other. We were looking at each other for the first time since the accident and I felt like a rabbit frozen in a car's headlights. But if she felt the same way, then I was the headlights for her.

"He's in a pretty good mood," I said.

"You must have told him something important."

"Naah. I never tell him anything."

"Me either."

"I don't tell anybody."

I must have broken some kind of rule by saying that,

35

because she tightened the grip on her books and narrowed her eyes. The next time she spoke it sounded really formal, like she was an heiress, or something. "I shouldn't be talking to you."

"I'm sorry," I said. "I didn't mean to upset you."

"I'm not upset," she snapped, but the way she tensed her shoulders said she was.

"Sometimes I'd *like* to tell somebody."

"I'm sure you could." This was definitely Ice Princess time.

"It's not that easy."

"At least you still have your parents." Each word was its own little dig.

"I'm sorry," I said again. "I . . . ," but everything was coming out wrong, so I shut up. Her eyes had begun to tear up a little. I was sorry I even noticed that, because it made her furious.

"Why am I even standing here?" she said, getting madder the whole time.

I thought about laying a hand on her arm, but it was like she knew that ahead of time and stepped away from me.

"I thought it might help if we could . . ."

". . . talk about it" never even reached my lips, because she looked at me like I was about to say "sleep together."

"He killed my mom and dad."

"I know," I said, "but it doesn't mean he's not dead, too."

"He deserves to be dead."

That was the worst thing anybody could say to me,

because sometimes I believed it myself. Ianetta stood in his doorway.

"Thanks for pointing that out," I said.

There was hardly anybody in the locker room when I got there, which was just as well, because I felt like starting a fight. Being the mature guy that I am, I took it out on my locker, slamming it open, slamming it closed, dropping a few books, the whole drill.

"Damn it!" I screamed and turned from the locker straight into the face of this teacher. At least I thought he was a teacher. He was young, maybe twenty-six or twenty-seven, not much taller than me, say five foot five. He had black curly hair and a high forehead. His mustache was bushy and he had green-brown eyes. I mostly remember the eyes because even that day they were sort of calming. Which was more than I could say for his words.

"Look, I just came from Ianetta," I said. "You can't send me back."

"I don't know who Ianetta is."

"Wish I had your luck."

"You're Bobby Connely, aren't you?" he asked. "I'm Sal Martinelli." He held out his hand, but mine were still shaking, so I just nodded.

"I hear you're a pretty good ballplayer," he said.

"I don't play. Anymore."

"I heard that, too," he said. "I was hoping I could change your mind."

"Why?"

"I just came from Mr. Kelsey's office," he said. "I'm Mr. Burke's replacement. I'm the new baseball coach."

He said it like he had to keep reminding himself. "Good luck with these stiffs," I said.

"No stiffs this year," he said. "Well, not many. Most of the team graduated. I'm going to be relying on a lot of the younger guys. I'd like you to think about coming out."

"No. No way."

"You ever heard of Kenny Bibb?"

"Yeah, black kid from Consolidated. People say he's gonna be the best shortstop since . . ." *Yeah, since.* "I'm not coming out."

"That's too bad. Kenny Bibb is. His family is moving into the district in a couple of weeks. I guess his dad is going to manage one of the banks around here."

For just a second or two, I let myself imagine what Martinelli wanted me to imagine: I dive into the hole for a grounder and snap it, on one knee, to Bibb covering second. He lets it go almost before he's got it. Double play, smooth as pouring a glass of milk.

"I don't mean to push," he said. "I just want you to know that I think you have a lot of player in you. It might do you some good."

"It didn't do my brother much good."

"You shouldn't blame that on baseball," he said.

"Yeah, well thanks for pointing that out. People are sharing all kinds of insights with me today."

"I hope I'll see you around," he said.

"Doubt it."

6

No-Name Park isn't really a park, which is probably why they never got around to naming it. The county just decided it was a good place to stick a couple of picnic tables and surround them with a split-rail fence. They cut down the trees near the top of the hill so you can see most of the Polywaxen Valley. It's not a lot to look at really, all carved up with quarries and dusty with smoke from the Ash, but sometimes, just being up that high seems peaceful. You can still hear the machinery hum, but not if you climb a tall tree.

I hiked up there on my way home from school because it seemed like the one place where I wouldn't have to worry about screwing up somebody's life. But when I broke through the trees and stepped over the fence, I saw that it was bad-guy time again. Sitting at a table, staring down into Ryder, was Annie Dunham. She saw me right away. We were twenty yards apart, but she seemed close enough to take a swing at me.

"Are you following me?" she called.

"No, I just came up to look at the town."

"Which one?"

"The old one."

I crossed the service road and sat down two tables to her right. For a while I tried picking out cars that I recognized on the streets in Ryder. Being around her was spooky, but I wasn't going to leave. I'd already cut out once for her sake. Which reminded me . . .

"What did you mean that day at the bus stop when you said, 'Thank you'?"

"I don't remember."

"Yes you do," I said. I guess our first conversation hadn't taught me any tact.

"You don't know what I remember."

"You remember everything you see me do and I remember everything I see you do because we're stuck with each other."

"Don't flatter yourself."

"It's not flattery. It's probably the opposite. Anyway, it's true, isn't it?"

"I wish it wasn't."

"So do I. Before, I hardly even *knew* you."

"You hardly even know me now."

"I mean before, I hardly even had to think about you."

"Oh, and now you do, right?"

"Yeah, all the time. I mean I pretty much divide the

place up, your places and my places, so you won't have to see me and I won't have to see you."

"Except for social studies," she said.

"I tried to switch out of it," I said, "but they wouldn't let me."

"I did, too."

"I think they think it's some kind of experiment, socialization of hostile people, or something like that. Like it's supposed to help us get used to . . ."

"You sound like Ianetta."

"He's not such a bad guy."

"He's the wrong one," she said.

"The wrong one for what?"

"Telling things to."

That was pretty much what I'd wanted to hear. Misery loves company and all that kind of thing. But now that she'd said it, I didn't know what to do. I couldn't just say, "Well, gee, we have a lot in common. Death for instance. Let's be buddies." In fact, I felt kind of bad for bothering her in the first place. It seemed like I should apologize.

"I know you hate me," I said. "I know this might be worse for you than it is for me, but I'm trying not to be a part of it. Okay?"

She didn't answer for a long time, but I waited her out. Silence is something I'm used to. When she started talking her hands framed her face like blinders.

"Doesn't it feel like you're dying sometimes?" she asked.

"Sometimes."

"Sometimes I feel like I should already be dead."

"Don't do it."

"I *can't* do it. I tried to make myself do it, but I can't."

I knew chuckling was the wrong response, but I couldn't stop myself. "What did you try?"

She looked at me like I'd just puked.

"No, serious. I tied this plastic bag over my head and all I got was a rash around my neck." I pulled down the collar of my shirt to show her what was left of the scar.

"That could be from a razor blade," she said.

"Right, my *monthly* shave."

Her face was back in the blinders. "I went up in the bell tower at Holy Angels," she said. "You can open the slats far enough to crawl out. I made it to the dome, but then I got chicken."

Holy Angels is the tallest building in Reese Point. Just the idea of her out on a ledge with one of those huge plaster saints scared the shit out of me. "You could have slipped or something," I said. She shrugged that off.

"I kept wondering what would happen inside your head if you changed your mind. What if you were on the way down and your whole life was flashing in front of your eyes and you thought of something great, or you remembered something you forgot to tell somebody, or you didn't know who would get your dog."

"I didn't know you had a dog." It was a stupid point to pick up on, but it seemed harmless.

"Cheever. My father named him after a writer he liked. He's just a mutt."

"The writer?"

That made her laugh a little. "I meant that I was glad

42

you ran out on that sub the other day instead of—you know."

"Oh. You're welcome."

She gave me the world's shortest smile. "I don't hate you. I just . . ."

"I was thinking about this the other day."

"About *this*?"

"About, you know, trying to talk to you. I didn't know how I was going to do it or even *if* I was going to do it, but— That's why I told Kerrins I had that doctor's appointment. I thought I'd miss your bus."

"You were going to take my bus?"

"I don't know. I probably would have chickened out."

"This is weird. Talking to you is weird."

"It's *not* weird. I mean *it's* weird, but we're not weird."

"What do you call a guy who ties a plastic bag around his neck and—what I did?"

"You ever tell anybody about that before?"

"No."

"Me either."

"How come you told *me*?" she asked.

" 'Cause I thought you'd know what it was like."

She looked at me for just a second, then stared back down into the streets. "I guess you were right," she said, and gathered up her books.

" 'Bye," I said.

" 'Bye."

She walked down the hill and took the Reese Point turn at the fork. This is sort of stupid, but I climbed a tree and watched her disappear among all the two-family homes.

43

Diving

We were playing Prisoner of War. Billy and Richie Munley had gone way out of bounds. They were hiding in one of the big cement pipes up beside the creek. Once I tracked them down, I broke off a scrawny birch branch to use for my gun. It would have been fun to charge their fort yelling, "Da-da-da-dah. Da-da-da-dah," but the object of the game was to capture them.

I snuck around behind the casing and climbed a little dirt mound so I could see inside. For the next five minutes I just lay there, feeling the whole time like I wanted to wet my pants. Billy and Richie were sitting on the floor staring at two girls from their fourth-grade class. All the girls had on were panties. Lynn Teague's were yellow. Karen Shaw's were blue.

Richie said something and the girls started giggling.

Then they took off their panties, too. Karen Shaw wiggled her bottom around and sang some playground song, but Lynn Teague just pressed her legs together. After a while they started to put their clothes back on. I saw their rear ends when they bent down.

"You can't tell anybody you saw us," Lynn Teague said.

"We promise," Billy said.

"We want you to show us, too," Karen Shaw said.

"Show us again and we'll show you."

The girls pulled their panties down around their ankles. When Richie told them to turn around, they did that too.

"Now you," Lynn Teague said. She sat down on the floor in her shirt and underwear.

My brother and Richie stood up and walked to the other side of the tube. They didn't take their pants off, just kind of pushed them down around their knees.

"They're in their underwear," Karen Shaw sang. "Now you have to show us your *things.*"

"No way," Billy said.

"You promised," Lynn Teague said.

Richie pulled his underwear down in the front for just a second. Billy did the same thing.

"That doesn't count," the girls said. Richie and Billy flashed them again.

Karen Shaw got up and stood in front of Richie. The next thing I knew she pulled down his shorts and was looking right at it. Lynn Teague did the same thing to Billy, only not for as long.

I should have sneaked back around the way I came, but

all I could think of was getting out of there fast. Sneaking down the dirt mound, I kicked loose a stone and started a landslide.

"Somebody's coming," Lynn Teague whispered. "Billy, oh my God, it's your brother." The girls tore out of the tube in their underwear and started winging stones at me. It must have taken Billy and Richie a couple of seconds to fix their pants, but pretty soon they were right on my tail.

"You're dead, Bobby," Richie yelled.

They were gaining pretty fast when I got to the creek, so I ran right in. The bottom was muddy and the water swirled around my knees. A couple of times I almost fell down. My pants stuck to my legs. Now I'm dead from Mom, too, I thought. The only good thing was that Billy and Richie stayed on the other side.

"You better not tell," my brother shouted, but pretty soon I couldn't hear him.

When my mother asked me what happened to my clothes I told her I fell in the creek playing Prisoner of War with Billy. We both got in trouble for that, but I kept the other stuff a secret.

7

He'd come home late once in a while from work or a meeting, but I always figured that was a good sign. "Some of the fellas were going over to Ernie's to get a drink, so I thought I'd go along for the company," he told me once after a Holy Name meeting.

My dad was aching for friends. After Billy died we didn't see much of the local baseball people anymore. Once he moved into the office at the Ash, he never saw his buddies in the plant, either.

Ever since the accident he'd become kind of a shadow, there and not there. Sometimes I swore he didn't know what was going on right in front of him. Or maybe he knew, but he couldn't get near the right kind of response. It always seemed like he had a lot to say, but it seemed like it would take an hour's worth of rambling for him to say it. I could see my dad wanting to have drinks with some-

47

body, but I was pretty surprised that anybody would want to have drinks with him. The more he stayed out late, the better I thought he was doing, which is Exhibit A in the case for me being stupid.

One night in early December he came home from Ernie's, put on some coffee, buttered a roll, and sat down in the kitchen with the high school sports pages. He read the high school sports about three times a day, like he was expecting a score to change or something. "Forest Grove's got quite a team this year," he'd say, or, "That little Gillespie kid sure can handle the ball." It drove me right up the wall. Pretty soon I'd be upstairs in bed, missing whatever was on the late movie. Not long after that, he'd follow.

I don't know how it started, or why it started on that particular night, but Dad raised his voice first.

"For Christ's sake, it was only the fellas from the Holy Name."

"I don't care if it was Monsignor Fadden," my mother said.

"Catherine, you make it seem like I stayed out all night."

"This isn't the first time," she said. "Don't you think I notice?"

"I didn't think it mattered," he said. "I don't come stumbling up the driveway."

"Bill, after everything that's happened . . ."

They must have made up after that because I didn't hear any more about it for almost a month. I just figured it was a little noise over a little drinking. Which is Exhibit B in the case for me being stupid.

Maybe you've never spent any time around a drinker. There's one thing about them that not too many people know. Drinkers are sneaky. I guess you learn that when you're my age. The older kids, who get the beer for you, don't want you to get caught, so they teach you these tricks. You can't really tell if they're scientific or anything, but it seems like they work.

You're supposed to drink milk before you go out, to coat your stomach. Then they tell you to moon the bottom of each beer because it's mostly spit by that point anyway. If you feel like puking it's better to stick your fingers down your throat and get it over with before you go home. As far as beer breath is concerned, mints and pizza are usually pretty helpful. The crucial thing is to take a couple of aspirins when you're done and drink about a gallon of water. That way, sometimes, you can skip the hangover.

It's a lot of trouble.

The only time I ever got caught drinking was also the last time my mother ever hit me. The freshman class had a keg party at Maloney Field on the first warm weekend last March. What I remember most about it was mud up around your ankles and all us guys jostling for position at the keg like we were fighting for a big rebound. Everybody wanted to be the first one to say, "God, I'm sooo drunk."

I'm still not clear on the advantages of chugging a full cup of beer, but I tried it that night and it was the straw that broke the camel's back, or upset the camel's stomach, or whatever.

Brian McHale walked me two miles home, but I was still so drunk when I got there that I couldn't even pretend I wasn't. My mother noticed it right off—*"Are you*

drunk?" "Yes."—and smacked me one right across the face. I think that surprised her as much as it surprised me, so just to prove she'd done it, she did it again.

All this happened while my brother was still alive, before I became a scholar about alcohol, so I didn't understand most of what she said next. Out in the kitchen she made me some tea and pulled a bottle of aspirin down from the cupboard.

"Do you remember your daddy's Uncle Tom?" she asked, which I did, but just vaguely. To me he was a red face, a loud voice, and a mouthful of bad teeth. "He was an alcoholic," my mother said. "And you know your Aunt Peg?"

I said I did. She was my dad's oldest sister. We didn't see her very often because she was in the Polywaxen County Mental Hospital.

"She's an alcoholic, too. Alcoholism is hereditary," she said. "It runs in your father's family."

"I'm not an alcoholic," I said.

"Have you ever been drunk before?"

"Once," I said. It was a lie by half.

"It can ruin your life. Ask your father."

At that point I had no idea what my father would know about it. I'd never even seen him drink a beer. I guess the "Why?" was all over my face.

"You didn't know your father had a drinking problem?"

Didn't know? I didn't believe her now that she was telling me. "He never gets drunk or anything," I said.

"He never does *now*. Thank God."

50

"When did he?"

"After he came home from the Army. Just before he and I began dating again."

"I thought you guys knew each other since like the second grade."

"We *knew* each other, but your father was a different person when he was a boy. He was like Billy in high school, the big baseball star. We've been lucky that Billy hasn't followed in his footsteps in other ways." She knocked on the wooden table.

My tongue was too numb for me to know if I'd bitten through it. I didn't squeal, though. Sometimes now I think that if I had squealed—but that's stupid. What my mother was saying meant almost nothing to me then. A dead great-uncle and a loony aunt. Alcoholism.

Everybody I knew drank on the weekends, my brother included. He just didn't get caught. I remember him coming into our room all juiced up with beer and gossip about which of the cheerleaders had a crush on him now. He was the first one who ever *gave* me a beer, or took me to a sleep-over party.

I'm not saying he was a wild man. Billy was my altar-boy partner until he was fifteen. We had a Sunday paper route together. He got low honors most of the way through school and was so polite with the relatives it made me sick. It's just that he liked to get a little drunk now and then. You don't have to be a maniac for this kind of stuff to happen to you.

"Do you remember when Grandma Connely died?" my mother asked.

51

"Not too much."

"You were only four then. You wouldn't remember your father drinking."

"I'm sorry," I said.

"I know you are. Let's not have this conversation again."

We never did. But of course everything she said that night has haunted me since the accident and I'm sure it has haunted her, too. After Billy died I was convinced that my mother was right about the Connelys. There was a devil, or something, in our blood and I was kind of relieved to hand myself over to it. I don't know if my father felt that way, but he handed himself over, too.

Exhibit C in the case for me being stupid is that I had no idea he was drinking heavily again. He could have maxed out Holy Name meetings for the rest of his life and I never would have caught on. The thing was, he wasn't much different toward us. A little more distant maybe, but he'd been so distant before that I couldn't tell. My mother could, though. I'm still not sure whether she knew something bad was going to happen, or if she just acted like she did, and ended up helping it happen.

Before everything went haywire my parents hardly ever fought, so I figured his night out with the Holy Name boys would be the end of it. But my father went along like nothing had ever been said. A few days later he brought home a six-pack with some groceries. On Friday he told her he was going to Ernie's that night to watch hoops on the big screen.

It was just after midnight when he came home. *The Treasure of the Sierra Madre* was on the All-Nighter, so

I sprawled out on the floor with a big bag of Doritos. He was a little buzzed, not shitfaced, just happy.

"Who won the game?" I asked.

"Sixers. What's on?"

"Bogart."

"Hey. 'Badges. We don't need no stinking badges.'"

"That's coming up."

"When did your mother go up?"

"I got home an hour ago. She was up there then."

I'm not sure what happened upstairs, but the bandits hadn't been gone long when Dad came back down, smiled this weak smile, and shuffled into the kitchen. *"A buttered roll, the high school sports, and thou,"* I thought to myself. But in a second I heard the familiar "pop" of somebody cracking open a beer. I don't know why that surprised me the way it did. I guess when he bought them he meant to drink them. But now he was actually doing it. In the house. With Mom upstairs. I sat there semi-stunned until I heard the rustle of her robe on the steps.

"Bobby, turn that off and get up to bed," she said. Her slippers made a whispering noise on the carpet.

Needless to say, I sort of lingered in the hallway. Dad was sitting at the table with a silver glint in his hand.

"You'll be right behind him," she said. Her voice was real flat. She could have been reading off a phone number.

Diving

Bottom of the sixth inning, one out, down by one run. Billy is on third base, I'm on first. This was right after I started Little League.

Coach Vukovich gave me the steal sign, but I knew I couldn't make it, so I stayed put. He looked pissed off and gave me the sign again on the next pitch. I was still afraid of making a mistake, though, so I didn't run.

"He wants you to steal, stupid," said Ned Boles, the first-base coach. "Go ahead, run." But I was only nine and the pitcher and catcher were both twelve. I knew dead meat when I smelled it, so I just froze.

The count must have been about 2 and 2 by that point. Even Billy was motioning for me to go, but I'd already made up my mind not to.

On the next pitch, whoever was hitting smacked a one-hopper right to the shortstop. He turned it into a double play and the game was over. The whole team was mad at me.

"Why didn't you run, ya big baby."

"You cost us the game, you little chicken."

Usually after we played I'd go up to the refreshment stand and buy pizza and a cream soda from my mother. But after that game, I didn't feel like being around anybody, so I just sat in the car until we were ready to leave.

Mom bought me shoestring licorice.

"You should have run," Billy said when he got in.

"They would have gotten me out."

"No, they wouldn't have. If they threw to second base then I would have scored."

This was a great thing to know, but at the time it just made me feel stupid for not knowing it sooner. When we got home I stayed in the car, figuring Billy would change his clothes and go out to play. Then I could have the room to myself.

Five minutes later he showed up on the porch. "Come on in," he said. "I'll show you what to do."

For the next half hour we sat at the kitchen table spreading out loose leaf. He drew little diagrams trying to explain when to run and when not to run. My mother said she wished Billy spent that much time on his schoolwork.

This was right around the time that Mom was showing microwave ovens to make extra money. When we were finished, Billy cooked me up a chicken patty. It came out dry, but I put a lot of catsup and mayonnaise on it and after that it tasted pretty good.

55

8

All this happened around the time that I started to pretend I had friends. There wasn't much trick to the first part of it. I'd just call my mother and ask if it was okay to eat over so-and-so's house. Usually she'd say yes. The hardest parts were mixing up the people so I wouldn't be expected to know too much about anybody, and finding something to do with my time. Mostly I went to the library. Sometimes I'd walk up to No-Name Park and sometimes I'd call the Cowboy.

Charley lived in about the littlest house in America. It was stuck on top of a small hill in the middle of this tree-stumped lot on the two-lane that ran from Reese Point to Mount Wilson. A red-ash driveway led up the slope of the front lawn. At the top of the hill sat a mint-green '62 Biscayne. That was the car he was teaching me to drive in. Beside it stood a small shed where he kept his cycle. The house itself had been painted almost the same shade as the car and was shaped like a small U with short arms.

I felt bad for the Cowboy whenever I went to his house because it seemed like such a depressing place to live. In the right arm of the U stood a small table and three rusty chairs. The refrigerator and stove were pushed against the wall behind them. The sink sat off to the left. He always kept the other arm of the U closed. "My chambers," Charley called it. The middle of the place was taken up mostly by stereo equipment, but he also had a couch and a coffee table.

There were records and tapes piled up everywhere. The Cowboy liked to say that within five minutes he could put his hands on any worthwhile rock album pressed in the last twenty-five years.

Sometimes, when we got high, Charley would put in a Time Capsule. The capsules were special tapes he made. Every song came from the same year. He'd play the music and tell me all the stuff that happened that year. Politics, books, movies, everything. "Try to imagine," he kept saying, and I would. It was like living in another time, even if it was a time you'd already lived in.

The Cowboy was a different person when he was narrating a Time Capsule. He'd get all charged up, like he was preaching a sermon.

Charley is one of those people who thinks the world will blow up any day now. He made it seem like Paradise Lost was the theme of every year since about 1952. It was depressing, but it was educational. That's why I know who Francis Gary Powers was and that U-2 was a plane before it was a band.

I went up to visit him the night after my dad opened the beer. We ordered a pizza with everything except the little fish on it, and ate ourselves into a stupor. After dinner I sat there staring at the ducks on a six-pack of Molson and pretending that I lived in a cabin beside some lake in Canada. Charley leafed through his albums.

"How's folks?" he said.

"Not so great. My dad's drinking and my mom's freaking out about it."

"How 'bout you?"

"I'm just trying to keep out of everybody's way."

He dropped *Darkness on the Edge of Town* onto the turntable. "Gotta match the music to the mood," he said, lighting a joint. But I didn't feel like smoking. I was already a little drunk, so I just tipped my head back and let the beat of "Badlands" rip through me.

Pretty soon I clenched my fists and my whole body was twitching in time. It almost felt like being in a fight. When the first chords of "Adam Raised a Cain" filled the house, Charley cranked up the volume and we screamed along:

> *"Born into this life paying*
> *For the sins of somebody else's past."*

After the guitar wail faded Charley turned down the sound. "That'll air your rage out," he said. He was sitting on the couch now. I was lying on the floor looking at the liner notes.

"So what else?" he asked, and opened the last two beers.

"Reese Point has a new baseball coach. He wants me to play."

"Gonna?"

"Right."

"Why not? Run around a little, get your rocks off beating on a ball. That's not so bad."

"Just gives everybody a chance to talk about my brother all over again."

"So, you play good, you rub everybody's nose in it. What are you afraid of?"

"Nothing. It's just—grotesque."

"Gro*tes*que," he said. "I'm talking baseball, this guy's talking vocabulary quiz."

"Fuck you," I said, laughing, and sailed a pillow at him. He swatted it down on the table, knocking over his beer.

"You little jerk," he said. "Now we have to go for more."

"Maybe you should drop me on the way," I said. "I'm pretty whipped and I'm trying to stay *way* out of trouble."

We bundled ourselves up and tramped out to the car. It was about five degrees, but the Biscayne's engine roared in the cold. "Best fifty dollars I ever spent," Charley said, backing down the driveway onto Mount Wilson Road.

"How's that class you're in with those people's daughter?"

"All right."

Mount Wilson Road winds like an old riverbed down into the Polywaxen Valley before heading back uphill to Reese Point. The road takes about one life per winter, but

59

Charley always attacked it like he was a slalom champ. The headlights of oncoming cars shone right in our faces. I thought about Annie Dunham and about being the rabbit, as well as the headlights.

"I talked to her," I said.

"Yeah?"

"Yeah, last week after school. She has a dog."

"She has a dog," Charley said pronouncing every word deliberately.

"Well, I don't want to get into it that much, all right?"

Charley eased the car off the road in front of a cranky-looking joint called Bullhead's. "Right out," he said, and left the engine running.

I was fiddling with the radio dial, trying to scare up something I could sing to, when the Cowboy came shooting down the stairs and yanked open the door. "Come here," he said. "Come on, hurry up," and ran back up the steps.

I caught him at the door. "Can you drive?" he asked.

"I can do what you taught me."

"That's good enough. Now listen: Your dad's in there and he's pretty loaded. They cut his drinks, so he's just sitting around. Nothing's going on. He's not bothering anybody, but a couple of the guys think he's pretty funny. We're just going to go in and get him out of there and you're gonna take him home."

Charley swung the door open before I had a chance to think. The room smelled like old smoke and stale beer. Something country was playing on the jukebox. Four or five guys leaned against the walls around the pool table. I found my father about two thirds of the way down the bar, with his chin propped on his left palm. He was reading the names stitched on a banner that hung from the ceiling and didn't notice me at first.

"Hi," I said, like we met this way all the time.

He turned slowly, looking me over. "Bobby," he said finally, like I was an old friend whose name he'd just remembered.

"Thought you might need a ride."

That's when the double-digit-IQ crowd opened fire. "Hey Boots, look at this. Little Junior here's come to take the big fish home," one of them called.

"Hey Junior, what are you doing in a bar? You ain't even old enough to jerk off."

My father was on his feet. He took a step in their direction, but I got in his way. "Let's go home, Dad," I said.

"Let's go home, Dad," one of the princes at the pool table said in a high-pitched voice.

My father tried to threaten them, but his speech was so thick I didn't even understand it myself.

"Blaughmul heent hee?" my friend Boots said. "Blaughmul heent hee." They were having a good laugh when Charley, who had been distracting the bartender, caught up with us. He fished Dad's car keys out of his pocket and handed them to me. Then he helped my father on with his coat and kept chattering until the three of us were nearly out the door.

"You all come back now," one of Boots's boys shouted.

Charley hopped into the Biscayne, which was still running, while Dad and I stutter-stepped across the ice to his Escort.

61

We've had the car just over four years now. It was the only new one Dad had ever owned. He taught Billy to drive in it. I always thought he'd teach me, too, but after what happened I could understand why he wasn't too hot on the idea. I learned what I know about driving from Charley on dirt roads and in parking lots. Good thing, too, I thought, palming the warm keys in my pocket.

My father got in on the passenger's side like there was nothing unusual about that. "Glad to see you," he said. But the opening of my performance didn't exactly inspire confidence. The engine roared like a race car because I started it with too much gas. Then I couldn't find the rear defroster. My feet wouldn't reach the pedals and I didn't know how to move the seat forward. Nothing like calling a little attention to the unusual here, I thought. I kept waiting for Dad to ask me where I'd learned to drive, but somehow it never came up.

When he finally spoke, what he said was: "Forest Grove's got a hell of a team this year." For the effect it had on me, he may as well have announced he was planning to jump out the door.

Recycling old small talk had to be a sign of mental illness, I thought. *Forest Grove's got a hell of a team.* Jesus.

"They beat Hildreth tonight by twenty-six," he said. "You should have seen that little Gillespie, penetration all night long. Zone, man-for-man, didn't matter."

"Good ballplayer, huh?" I was hoping that if he kept talking I'd figure out what he was talking about.

"Oh yeah. I'd say he and that Shelp boy from Temple Pass are the best guards in the conference. Best ones I've

62

seen anyway. Course the Shelp boy is bigger. He'll do well in college. But I'll take Gillespie on my team. He's a world-beater."

"You go to a lot of games," I said matter-of-factly, although it was a revelation to me.

"Over the last two, three weeks," he said. "Does me good to see the boys out there on the court. You never really cared for basketball much, did you?"

"Naah. Too short. No shot."

"It wasn't your brother's game, either. He played tough defense, though. I think he had a shot to start this year."

Dad cracked the window and tilted his face into the stream of cold air. "You know, I sit up there and watch the Gillespies and the Shelps and the rest of those boys, and I wonder how he would have done out there."

"I'm sure he would have done great," I said and heard my voice break.

That was like the hypnotist snapping his fingers. Dad heard it and buried his face in his hands. "I can't go home like this," he said after a while, but I let it ride.

Turning the car onto Hollow Hill Road, I felt as relieved as I'd ever been. But when I pulled up in front of the house, my father said, "I can't go in like this. Take me to my sister's."

"Dad, it's almost midnight. Aunt Gracie lives thirty miles from here." I sounded pretty reasonable for somebody in a panic. He was in no shape to drive to Darden and neither was I.

"Maybe we can get some coffee," he said.

"Look, the lights are out. Mom's probably asleep."

63

"Your mother doesn't sleep."

I knew he was right about that, so I shifted into drive and gave it a little gas.

I had just the spot. The Blue Shutter Diner, which no longer has any shutters at all, is only about six blocks from our house. There wasn't much of a crowd inside. The Shutter stays open until four A.M. and I don't think anybody goes in there until after the bars close at two. We dropped into a booth in the rear corner and ordered coffee for him and tea for me.

The diner lights are a little on the harsh side. Not real flattering if your complexion has the bluish-green tint my dad's did that night. "Maybe you should eat something," I said to him when the waitress walked away.

"Look at *you* taking care of *me*," he said. "I sure have gotten things backward."

"What about some fries?"

Dad shook his head, glanced at me, and then stared out the window. I could tell he was looking for the words to say something difficult, and I hoped he wouldn't find them.

When people have that look on their faces the news is never good. Either it is a confession that will change the way you look at them, or it is a fact that will change the way you look at everything else. You wish that you could stop them, but their fear of keeping it inside is greater than your fear of hearing it. People who know are always in control, especially if what they know is horrible.

My father rolled a spoon gently between his fingers.

What he finally said was: "Bobby, whatever happens with us, don't hate me for what I've done."

This was before I knew there was a mystery on, so I didn't take that as a clue.

"Jesus, Dad," I said, "don't be so hard on yourself. You're not the first guy to have one too many in Bullhead's."

But he was making his own plans and paying no attention.

In the parking lot Dad asked me for the keys. I knew I shouldn't have given them to him, but there aren't a lot of arguments for an underage kid to use when his father says he wants to drive home. It was only six blocks, I thought, maybe not enough time to crash.

In a way, I guess I was right. The drive was no problem. But when we reached the house, he pulled up at the curb instead of swinging into the driveway. "Why don't you go on in," he said. "I'm going to spend the night at Aunt Gracie's."

Of all the times I've felt alone since my brother died, I never felt as desperate about it as I did right then. Before, I could just fetus up and let it wash over me, but this time I was supposed to *do* something.

"That's probably not a good idea," I said, trying to buy some time.

"No, it's okay. I'm fine now," he said.

"Dad, you're not fine. Come on in. Mom won't . . ."

"Go in the house and we'll talk about it tomorrow."

"Let me drive you."

"Your mother would kill me if . . ."

"Well, you're going to kill yourself and God knows who else if you go out on the road like this."

Kill was the word that beat me. Everything after that came out kind of high-pitched and sobby, like the way that guy had imitated me in the bar.

"Now stop that," my father said. "Nobody's going to get killed. Go on in, and if your Mom asks, tell her I've gone to Gracie's and tell her I'm fine."

"She won't believe me."

"Sure she will."

"She's not stupid, you know. What do you think, everybody's stupid?"

He reached over to put a hand on my shoulder and suddenly things started to happen. I swatted his arm away and he pulled back. That's when I saw my chance and lunged for the keys.

Dad grabbed my arms. We were wrestling. I knew he was still drunk then, because I was holding my own.

He got the keys away from me, but I dove on him again. When he pushed me back into the horn, it let out a loud blast. *That was it.* I spun, grabbed the horn, and squeezed it with all my might.

Dad tried to pry my fingers off, but with gloves on, he couldn't get a grip. Finally I felt a sharp pain in my ribs, and a jolt to the shoulder knocked me back against the door. The lights were on up and down the block. I imagined the rustle of Mom's robe and the whisk of her slippers on the carpet.

Mr. Williver came out on the porch and I sank down in the seat so he couldn't see me. "Sorry, Paul," my dad said. "Some kind of short in the horn. I yanked the wire."

No one else came out on their porch except my mother. Dad stepped over the hedge and crossed the yard. "It's all right," I heard him say. She must have known he was drunk, because she didn't answer, just hung her head and grabbed the railing.

If I'd been thinking, I would have stayed low on the seat and hoped she never saw me. Fifteen minutes later I could have waltzed in just a little late and hurried right up to bed. But I was nauseous and my shoulder ached. That wasn't the whole thing, either. My mother wouldn't let my father hurt me if he was still mad.

"Oh my God," she said when I stepped out onto the street.

Being the two brave men we were, neither of us made a move to comfort her. I watched him watch her.

They sent me straight upstairs. There wasn't any yelling, so I never heard how it happened. But when I woke up the next morning, my father was gone.

Diving

Confirmation was the first thing that we did at the same time. The bishop came to St. Peter's when I was eleven and Billy was thirteen. Every day we sat in the same class after school memorizing answers in a catechism. We got measured for our robes together and did our community service in the same place. Mom and Dad even let us choose the restaurant we went to that night. It was pretty great.

The only hard part was deciding on another name. We already had two each, but I could see how it was smart to line up as many patron saints as possible.

I was going to take James since Uncle Jimmy was my sponsor. Billy didn't want me to, though, because then Mom would have made him take Aloysius, after his sponsor, who was her cousin.

"I was thinking about Michael," I said one day walking home from class.

"Michael isn't too bad," Billy said. "Maybe I'll take it, too."

"We can't both."

"Who said?"

"Better ask Mom."

He didn't exactly ask. When dinner was over he said, "Bobby and I decided that we both want our confirmation name to be Michael."

They didn't like it at first, but he'd caught them off guard, so neither of them had anything to say. Mom stopped for a couple of seconds in the middle of clearing away the dishes to think about it. Dad looked into his coffee cup like he was expecting to find a better name written on the bottom.

"Do you *know* anybody named Michael?" Dad asked.

"Well," Billy said, "we'll know each other."

That was a good one. I wished I'd thought of it. But I didn't know how good a one it was until I noticed my mother standing over by the sink, looking out the window like she was going to cry from happiness.

Once in a while we would write each other notes or birthday cards using our full names. It was like we were more brothers for having the same middle name, which we picked out, than the same last name, which we didn't.

9

My mother was the one who told me about sex. I think she was the one who told Billy too, but he never let on. Mom is a natural when it comes to teaching. She never said, "Trust me," to dodge a tough question, or "You're too young to understand," even when we were. On the morning my father left, though, she didn't have too much to say.

I didn't know he was *gone* gone at first, I just knew he wasn't home. "Where's Dad?" I asked, munching on my cereal. Mom set a brochure on the table beside my juice glass and pretended she was busy in the cupboards.

The place was called St. Joseph's and it was in this scruffy little mountain town named White Birch Falls, which was way out in the central part of the state. "A six-week rehabilitation program . . ." is what caught my eye.

"*Six* weeks?"

"It's very comprehensive," my mother said.

I was already starting to think that Dad wouldn't have left if Mom hadn't sent him away, and that maybe she'd sent him away because of what happened with me, the night before.

"Daddy's not an alcoholic," I said.

"We don't need to argue about the names we call it, Bobby. Your father's drinking has been getting worse since—for some time now and he's gone to get help."

"I don't think he has a problem," I said, which wasn't exactly true. The night before, scared shitless in the passenger seat, I knew he had a problem. But Mom wouldn't let the guy up. Every time he drew a deep breath she'd be standing there asking him how he could inhale when their oldest son was dead.

"He *has* a problem," she said. "And if you're not careful you'll have a problem, too. I'd like to know what you were doing in that bar last night?"

"A friend of mine told me I should go in and get Dad."

"And of course your friend went in there to buy Coke."

"No, Mom, I guess he went in there to get some beer."

"You guess. Bobby, I don't want you going around with boys who are drinking beer."

"Jesus Christ, Mom, if it wasn't for Charley he would have driven all the way home from Mount Wilson drunk," I said. Since I was already in trouble from the first Jesus Christ, I figured I might as well get the rest of it out of my system. "Charley's my friend. He's just about the only friend I have and I don't care what you think about him."

She paused for a couple of seconds, letting me see how cool she was. "You will not go around drinking beer," she said. "And if you don't have enough character to stop it by yourself, I'll stop it for you. Now I want you in this house by nine o'clock on weekend nights and I want you home right after school. And don't you *ever* speak to me like that again."

Dad gets sent away to jail. I stay home in jail. Mom holds the keys. This hole was getting too deep to crawl out of. Not being able to see Charley was like having dirt shoveled in on top of me.

"I'll talk like that all I want," I shouted, picking up the brochure and flinging it at her feet. "Jesus Christ. Jesus Christ. Jesus *Fucking* Christ." I remember pronouncing the "g" real hard, like that made it a nicer word to shout at your mother.

"You know what, Mom, I don't think Dad has a problem. I think *you* have a problem. You have a problem and you're taking it out on us. Every little thing the guy does around here is wrong by you, but he's just trying to live. If you wanna curl up and die, go ahead. But we wanna live."

My jacket hung by the door and I grabbed it on the way out. She didn't have a chance to say anything, assuming that you have something to say after your only son tells you it's okay for you to curl up and die.

I banged out the door, jumped down the stairs, hopped the fence into Webb's yard, and sprinted out onto Cooper Avenue. In about three minutes I was at the center of town. There is not enough room around here for me to run

72

it out of my system when I get pissed off. There's probably not enough room in the state.

I sank down on a bus-stop bench on South Main Street and tried to figure out what to do next. Normally I would have called the Cowboy, but if I told him what had happened, I was afraid he wouldn't let me hang around with him anymore. I thought about tipping over all the garbage cans on Main Street and making the police chase me down, but all the Reese Point cops are fat and they probably wouldn't have been able to catch up.

When I went to the pay phone, I acted like I knew *exactly* what I was doing, even though I hadn't thought about it at all. Even though, if I had thought about it, I probably would have realized it was crazy.

"Reese Point," I said to the operator. "McDonough. Richard on Willow."

Her aunt answered, and when she asked who was calling, an easy enough question, I froze up. "B-Brian. Brian McHale."

"Oh, yes, Brian from *R*yder. It's nice of you to call, Brian. You know she misses her Ryder friends very much. Annie. Annie, it's Brian McHale from *R*yder."

Great, I thought to myself. Just great. She's going to come to the phone all hepped up to talk to somebody from *R*yder and end up with Dial-a-Ghost. But her hello wasn't all that enthusiastic.

"Hi, it's not Brian McHale," I said, and hoped she'd recognize my voice.

"Why are you calling?" she asked.

73

Another reasonable question I was totally unprepared for. "Uhm, I, I guess I just wanted to talk to you."

"Why now?"

"Something happened. My dad got sent away. Or he left. Whatever. He's not home."

"Where did he go?"

"Someplace in the mountains. I think my mom sent him to a drunk farm. We got into a fight about it and I ran out the door. Not too cool, huh?"

"Where are you?"

"In a phone booth at Cooper and South Main, near the dry cleaners."

"I don't know what you want me to do," she said.

"I just wanted to talk," I said. "I wanted to figure it out with somebody."

"I think we have to figure it out for ourselves," she said. That didn't seem possible, but I didn't say so. "Where are you going to go?" she asked after the line had been quiet for a while.

"I don't know, walking. Up the park. Down the river. California, someplace."

"I'm sorry."

"Yeah, sorry to bother you. You better make up a good story to tell your aunt."

"She's probably in the other room ecstatic," she said. "She probably thinks I have a *date*. Aunt Patty thinks the world would be perfect if I'd start a new social life."

"You still have your Ryder friends, don't you?" I asked.

"Yeah, sort of, but I can tell nobody knows what to say to me. Everybody's really nice, but I feel like I make them sad and that makes *me* sad."

"Yeah, so you stay away from people," I said.

"For a while. But then you're just, you know, by yourself and it feels like you're shrinking."

"Come for a walk," I said.

"I shouldn't."

"I won't make you shrink. You can tell your aunt you're meeting a boy for lunch."

"I shouldn't."

"I'll wait for you at No-Name Park."

"Don't hate me if I'm not there."

"I won't hate you."

I hung up the phone and crossed the street to buy two cups of tea and a coffee, to go. It was clear and cold that morning and there wasn't any wind yet. Main Street was just waking up. A lot of old people in dark coats moved in and out of the shops. At the corner of Rock Cut Road a horde of little kids rode sleds and coasters down the hill.

In Ryder we used to go sledding on a hill that led down into an empty lot across from the Ash. Billy and I would lie one on top of the other for extra speed. When we got going as fast as possible, the guy on top would pretend he'd been shot and roll off. We were going to be stuntmen.

There might have been a few kids my age there that day, but I didn't feel like we lived in the same world. Watching them all shoot down the hill was probably the first time I understood that something about my life was over with.

I figured I'd get to the park before Annie, so I picked out a bench with a good view of both towns and fixed a cup of tea. I tried to think about what I would say to her when she showed up.

I miss my dad, even though he only left this morning.

I almost feel like I miss my mom, even though I just ran out on her half an hour ago. I hate Dad for hurting Mom, 'cause I love Mom. But I hate Mom for hurting Dad, 'cause I love Dad. Maybe she wouldn't want to talk about all this Mom and Dad stuff anyway.

After I finished the tea I got a little itchy wondering if she'd show up, so I climbed a tree and checked out Rock Cut Road. Nothing. It had never occurred to me that she wouldn't come, but now that she hadn't, I felt stupid for ever thinking she would. The slightest wind blew and the branches began to shake. I held on tighter for a while, but then gave up and climbed back down.

Just as I dropped from the bottom branch she appeared at the top of the sled paths.

"Tree house?" she said.

"No, I, ah, was looking for you."

She nodded like guys climbed trees to look for her all the time and sat down at the table. "I almost didn't come," she said.

"I got you a cup of coffee. There's cream and stuff in the bag."

"Thanks. It's chilly."

"Good weather for sleigh riding."

"Did you see all those little kids down there?" she asked. "They're so cute I could just . . . *Yeish.* Strong coffee!"

"Put some more cream in it."

"I can't; it makes me fat."

"You're kidding me. You're not fat."

"I am. I gained a pound this week."

"A pound? One pound?" I puffed up my cheeks and

held out my arms like I was carrying this enormous stomach. She laughed, so I walked around like that. "I'm Dumbo Dunham."

"Okay, okay," she said, dumping cream into the coffee. "There, satisfied?"

"Yeah, satisfied." I sat down feeling twitchy. For a few seconds I hadn't even thought about my parents.

"What happened with your dad?" she asked.

I shrugged and made a face like "Those are the breaks." I wanted to talk, I just didn't know how to go about it.

"Come on," she said. She was looking right at me then, or maybe it would be better to say she was looking right into me, because the look didn't stop where our eyes met. It kept on going, kind of shimmying through my body, with more shimmy at some parts than others. It was the kind of look that wakes up your whole self, and it doesn't matter that the person giving it to you doesn't intend it that way. All they want is to let you know that for a little while you are safe with them. But even if you know that, the look shimmies through you just the same.

I started to tell about the night before and the six-packs and the Holy Name and all the hard-drinking Irish Connelys, until I was sure I'd turned them into sitcom characters. She sat with her hands around her coffee. After a while she let off looking at me, but she kept on listening. I could see that in her face. Sometimes it seemed like listening to this was harder for her than living through it had been for me.

"Is it okay to visit him?" she asked when I finished.

"I don't know. I didn't really read past the first couple of lines."

"You should visit him," she said. "You should because the longer you go without seeing him, the harder it will be when you *do* see him and maybe something will even get lost about the way things were. And once it gets lost, you won't be able to get it back."

I guess I knew that she wasn't talking about something that might happen to me, but something that had already happened to her. And I guess she knew I knew it, because she sank back, slid her hands off the table, and folded them in her lap.

"What's the matter?" I asked. She didn't answer, just shook her head. "I won't make you shrink," I said. But that didn't help. She sat so still I got scared she would shrink.

Normally I'm not a touchy-feely person, but all I could think to do was hug her. I didn't exactly do that. I just sort of put my hand on her shoulder and patted it. She didn't exactly hug me back, just leaned so that her head rested against the top of my arm, where the muscles would be, if I had any.

"The night that . . . the last night I saw my parents we had a fight," she said. "I wanted to stay at Eileen Foley's and they made me go to Uncle Dick and Aunt Patty's. I told them I hated going to Uncle Dick and Aunt Patty's and that I wanted to go to the sleep-over, but my mother said there would be plenty of time for that when I was older. I said I was sick of them treating me like a child. Then my father beeped the horn and the last thing my mother said to me was that I better stop acting like one."

"That was the *last* thing?" I whispered.

"Not the very last. My father said, 'Good night, sweetheart. Try to have a good time.' That was the very last thing. Then I went inside and acted like everything was okay. And that's what I'm still trying to do."

I really did hug her after that and she buried her face in my jacket. Maybe we would have stayed that way for a long time. Maybe we would even have kissed. But neither of those things happened because right then a car full of kids cruised through honking their horn and shouting stuff like "Go for it," and "Hey, you gettin' any?" and "Pump her once for me." Every now and then something like that happens and it makes you ashamed of being a guy.

We threw away the rest of our drinks and headed back down Rock Cut Road. By the time we got to the bottom of the hill, there wasn't anything dramatic going on. I guess you could say we pulled ourselves together, but maybe you would just say we pulled back. We were just standing around with nothing else to do. It still felt pretty good being with her.

"Come down by the river," I said.

"It's too cold."

"We'll go somewhere else."

"Like where?"

"I don't know, for lunch. I have about three fifty. We could eat at Tony G.'s."

"You know, I don't think it's a very good idea for people to know I am talking to you."

"Why not?"

"Well, my aunt, for one thing, would go crazy about it. And if people knew, then school would be even worse, if that's possible."

She was right, but I had no place to go and she didn't seem to either. As soon as she walked away I'd have to deal with my mother and all the fighting would start again. "What about the movies?" I said.

"People will see us."

"It's dark."

"People will see us coming and going."

"Wait a minute. You go in before me. Sit on the right side in near the wall. I'll come in about five minutes later. No one will know. No one goes to Saturday matinees anymore anyway."

"And leave before me, too," she said.

"Okay."

"And don't sit next to me, sit behind me."

"Okay. Okay."

"What's playing?"

"I don't know, but let's go anyway."

"Stand right there for five minutes," she said, and began skittering down the walk. She hadn't gone far when she spun around. Chickened out, I thought.

"Do you like butter on your popcorn?" she called.

I said yeah.

She bought a big bucket and sat flush against the wall. All through the movie we slid it back and forth between us.

10

When we lived in Ryder my Mom gave out Communion at the five-o'clock Mass on Saturdays. About once a month my father would do a reading. A couple of times, when Billy and I were still altar boys, all four of us were up there together.

I'm not very spiritual. I don't lie awake at night thinking that God's up there listening to me kick around my problems like the Big Shrink in the Sky. But for some reason I never minded going to church. Billy always said that was because it was my only excuse to sing in public, but I think I just liked seeing everybody get together. That is also what I like about ball games and beer parties, but those are different stories. Anyway, it's possible that I didn't like church as much then as I remember liking it now. The four of us were together then. I don't know if we were blessed, but at least we were safe.

After we moved to Reese Point we joined Holy Angels, but they never had the hold on us that St. Pete's did. My parents still went to the Holy Name and Altar and Rosary meetings, but I think that's because they considered it mandatory, like Sunday Mass. And I kept on going to church because it was what I had always done. I didn't get anything out of it anymore, but I didn't feel like giving it up, either.

The first thing my mother asked me when I walked in the door that Saturday was whether I was going to the five-o'clock Mass with her. I said I was.

"Maybe you should make a good confession, too," she said. That was code for "You better apologize, young man." But I knew that would lead to a scene and I didn't think I could handle it yet.

I am not so hot on Confession. Of all the sacraments I've had, which is four of the seven, Confession is my least favorite. I feel like I spend half my time telling people what's wrong with me as it is. I'm like a soup kitchen for guilt and they just keep lining up out there. Shrinks, parents, teachers, priests. Besides, God already knows, so what's the point?

The thing was that after talking to Annie, I'd made up my mind to get along with Mom. So if she wanted me to go to Confession, I'd go. Maybe then *she'd* forgive me too. I yelled up the stairs that that was a good idea and why didn't I meet her at church. But she said no, that she was going too and we could ride down together.

"I'll go warm up the car," I said. I liked playing with the car, but I was also looking for an excuse to put off facing her.

"Where did you go?" she asked when she got in.

"For a walk and then to the movies."

"By yourself?"

"I sat in the back," I said, dodging the question. It was sort of fun having a secret.

"Bobby, I'm sorry you can't see your friends," she said.

"It's all right." That wasn't really true, but I didn't want to get into another fight. "Can we go visit Dad?"

"Not for three weeks," she said. "It's part of the program. In three weeks they have an open weekend. The spouses go up on Friday night and then on Saturday there's a barbecue for the families."

"That sounds great," I said. "It sounds long, but it sounds great." That just sort of sat there waiting for a follow-up, so finally I blurted it out. "I'm sorry I yelled at you," I said. "I didn't mean it."

"You were upset," she said.

"I didn't mean it. I really didn't."

The church was practically empty when we got there, except for two or three people standing outside each confessional. I was relieved to see that both boxes were in business, because that meant I wouldn't have to go to Monsignor Fadden. He was one of those old-school guys who wanted you to remember how many times you committed every sin. Then, when you were done, if you were a young guy, he asked you if you beat off. He didn't say it like that, but no matter how he put it, it was still none of his business.

I know priests aren't supposed to talk about what they hear in the confessional. When I was a kid I saw that movie about the one who went to jail instead of squealing

83

on the murderer. But I always imagined these guys pushing their chairs back from the dinner table and filling each other in on who was yanking it and who wasn't.

I liked to go to Father Streeter. You probably could have walked in there and said, "Well, Father, I'm messing up all over the damn place" and he would have said, "I'm sure you're under a lot of stress. Say one Our Father and hang in there."

I tried to give the guy a little more to work with than that, so he could muster up a real forgiveness, but lately it's been the same old stuff—fights at school, fights at home, disobeying teachers, getting drunk.

I feel guilty for not having more interesting sins. I mean the guy is in this dark little room for two or three hours with people whispering at him. The least you can do is keep him entertained. But then if you made something up you'd just have to say your penance and get right back on the end of the line. "Father, that story I just told you about myself and those girls in the Blessed Virgin's Sodality—it was made up for your amusement, Father. Especially the part about the syrup." Then he'd probably hit you with a penance that would keep you on your knees for a week.

So I told Father Streeter my boring sins and he told me to be kind to my parents and say three Hail Marys and three Glory Bes.

When I came out, my mother was already in a pew with her head bowed and her hands folded. She didn't look up when I knelt down beside her and I didn't look up until I finished my prayers.

By that time, the organist had already begun to murder

the entrance hymn and the whole congregation was moaning along. Except for my mother. Mom has this clear strong voice, which is where my allegedly clear strong voice allegedly comes from. She sang like none of the bad singing around her made any difference as long as she sang well. To look at her you would have sworn that while she was singing, everything was okay. That seemed like a pretty good deal, so I started singing too. When she heard my voice joining hers, she smiled like she might even have been proud of me.

Later on, at the Sign of Peace, we kissed each other on the cheek. I had a good feeling for a couple of hours after that, but then I started to wonder if it was really so easy to get your sins forgiven.

Diving

People thought Billy and I looked cute together, or something, when we were altar boys. They were always asking us to serve weddings on Saturday mornings, which was fine with us, because you usually got paid. After we were finished, two sacristy girls came in to dust and lay out the new altar cloths.

One of the girls was Katie Blanken and I think Billy had a crush on her. He decided we should hide in the basement one Saturday and jump out at them when they came down. I don't think it was much of a surprise, because they started whispering to each other on the stairs. When we jumped out, they charged right back at us, and started wrestling us up against the wall.

"You're the little one," Jeannie Riley said. "I can take care of you."

That was pretty much my first encounter with a girl

who wanted to get her hands on me as badly as I wanted to get my hands on her. After groping around with us for a while, they broke away and ran upstairs. Katie sneaked out toward the altar, but Billy followed her. Jeannie hid in the vestment closet.

As soon as I closed the door behind me, she jumped out and starting tickling me. I spun around and tickled her back. Pretty soon, we were reeling through the vestments and stoles and all the other stuff that priests wear. I was stronger, so I got behind her and started feeling her breasts. They were small, but they were there, and they were the first ones I'd ever touched.

Everything was okay until I tried to put my hand inside her shirt—then she stomped down on my feet and elbowed me in the ribs. I let go right away and she tore out of the closet. I was about to tear out after her when the sacristy door swung open.

"Hello, Jeanne Marie," I heard Monsignor Bryant say.

"Good morning, monsignor."

"Where's your partner today?"

Katie and my brother must have walked in off the altar right around then.

"Well, hello, Kathleen," he said. "Mr. Connely, what's your business here?"

"We forgot our cassocks," I heard Billy say.

"So you came to get them by way of the altar?"

"No, monsignor," he said. "I was helping her."

"There was something I couldn't reach," Katie Blanken said.

The closet door swung open and I held my breath waiting to see who it would be. Billy nearly screamed when he saw me. I didn't want to give him the cassocks, because they were my only excuse for being in there, but finally I did.

After he'd gone monsignor started joking around with the girls about who their boyfriends were. Priests are a lot nicer to girls than they are to guys. "Well, young ladies, and I hope you are behaving like young ladies," he said, "I'm on my way to say a Mass at the convent. I'll be out of your way as soon as I select my wardrobe."

I'd been listening at the door, but now I scooted to the back of the closet and hid in the rose vestments that only get worn one Sunday each Lent.

"Let's see," Monsignor Bryant said, "I'll need an alb and this and— Now who knocked these stoles down?"

I thought I was dead. I figured that when he picked them up, he'd see my feet and excommunicate me, because you had to figure that feeling up sacristy girls was a mortal sin.

But Monsignor Bryant was a porky guy and he wasn't too hot on bending down. "Oh, here's one," he said. "Jeanne Marie, can you come in here and pick up these stoles?"

She practically sprinted into the closet, and kept him busy with "Yes, monsignor," until he was safely out of the church. We didn't make a sound until his car started. Then we shut the door and fell down laughing.

11

Just because my mother and I were getting along didn't mean I wasn't grounded. I came straight home from school every day and finished all my homework because there was nothing better to do. But every night, around ten or ten thirty, when my mother was in bed, I'd call Annie Dunham. She had a phone in her room and she always answered it on the first ring. Most times we'd talk about home, or school, everyday stuff, but sometimes we'd get into where we wanted to go to college—she said Penn; I said DSU—or what we wanted to be when we grew up—she said a lawyer; I said a sportscaster. Tuesday night she was all revved up.

"My Uncle Dick said it's okay if I take driving lessons," she said. "They are going to let me get my license."

"That's great. I didn't even know you were sixteen."

"Just before Christmas," she said.

"You're older than me."

"And more mature. When's yours?"

"Next week."

"You're kidding. When?"

"I'm not telling."

"Come on, when?"

"Over the weekend, that's all I'm saying."

"Then you can get your license, too. Won't it be great to be able to go places?"

"Yeah," I said, although the idea of going someplace with her had never occurred to me.

"Uh-oh. Aunt P. just looked in here again. I think I'm about to get the third degree. Better go."

"Okay, see you tomorrow."

For a long time I lay still, thinking about going places with Annie Dunham. Where would we go? Out in the country? Up to the falls? Into Darden to see movies, or the orchestra, or the campus? God, it would be great. Philadelphia? New York City? Washington, D.C.?

I'm not speaking from experience here, but it seems to me that getting a driver's license has more to do with growing up than getting laid does. Having a driver's license made getting laid possible for a lot of kids, but getting laid didn't mean you could drive a car. A license didn't only change your situation, it changed you. As soon as you sat behind the wheel, the car turned into your apartment. For the first time, you could be like a private person. The stuff you did and the places you went in your car, they were your secrets. And if somebody found them out, *"Hey, man, we're out of here."* In a car, you can always escape.

That is what I was thinking on this happy little downhill run, which is probably why I don't trust happiness. Sooner or later, your memory starts throwing up trees in your path, and when you crash, you are much worse off than if you'd never run at all. I was lying there thinking about how you can always escape with a car, when I thought about my brother and what had inescapably happened to him.

That was the trouble with happiness. It was also the trouble with talking to Annie Dunham. She was like a sanctuary you could only visit for a little while. Then, when you got kicked out, the world looked uglier than it did before.

"This is never going to go away," I said to myself. "Don't forget it."

For two days I didn't catch her eye in social studies and I didn't call her on the phone in her room.

On Friday a note in her handwriting fell out of my locker: "Bobby, is something the matter? I feel like you are mad at me. Can we please talk?! I'm baby-sitting at the Cosparos' tonight, 318 Putnam. Maybe you could come over or call me. I don't know the number, but it is in the book. If you come use the side porch. *Please* let me know what is going on!! Annie."

I didn't plan on going. I thought I'd do my homework and watch TV until I got sleepy. Then maybe I'd read something. Or maybe I'd just sit around and be disgusted that my birthday was the next day. This was the first one since Billy died and now Dad wasn't going to be home either. We used to make a pretty big deal out of birthdays, but this year I knew nobody would want to, least of all me.

91

When I get into a good self-pitying funk, I don't mind pitying other people, too. We all seem like the helpless furry animals in children's stories. So I was lying around, thinking about what a bad deal the world had given me and Mom and Dad, when I realized that the list of people I worried about had grown. Until a week ago, I could have cut it off right there, but now, without my even knowing it, Annie Dunham was on it, too. And among the bad deals she'd been given was the one I was giving her right that second.

I felt responsible for her, but I didn't want that. I had too much trouble looking out for myself. So I pulled on my jacket, sneaked very quietly out the back door, and went over to the Cosparos' house to tell her so.

The Cosparos have a dog, which I was glad about, because it gave me something to do with my hands when she opened the door looking hurt. It was only eight thirty, but the four-year-old was already asleep. I would have been glad to play around with the dog for a while, but she said, "Bruno. Home." Bruno, who looked more like a Max, gave me the sad eye, and moped out into the kitchen.

"I didn't think you'd come," she said.

"I wasn't sure I would either."

She asked me if I wanted a Coke and I said no.

"I'm really mad about this, you know," she said. "I'm really hurt."

"I'm sorry."

"Don't tell me you're sorry. Just tell me why. What happened?"

"Nothing. Nothing happened exactly."

"Oh, that's great. Nothing happened. You just completely stopped talking to me, but nothing happened. That's great."

She was hurt more than I knew I could hurt her. "Did you ever have a hangover?" I asked.

"Once. What's that got to do with it?"

"Really?"

"Yes. One time. At Dorothy Hopkins's sleep-over. We had sloe gin fizzes and I got a hangover."

"Sloe gin? Well, that's what it's like when I talk to you. Everything is great when I'm doing it. We're gonna go to the movies. We're gonna take a trip. You're gonna get your driver's license. Everything is great. I feel better than I am. Then we stop talking and I just go sinking back into it and everything isn't great. It's worse than it was before."

"I make things worse for you?" she said.

"No. *You* don't, but getting to feel good does. It's like it's a lie and then when the truth comes out, it hurts worse than it did before."

She wasn't crying, but she looked like she might. Her voice got raspy and every once in a while it broke. "You said you wanted to figure it out," she said.

"I do."

"You don't. You want to talk about it and fool around about it so that it seems like it goes away, but you don't want to *do* anything about it. *You're afraid.*"

That was probably true, but I didn't feel like admitting it. "What am I afraid of?"

"Everything. You're afraid of talking in class. You're afraid of learning to drive. You're too afraid to go out for baseball and now you're afraid of me."

93

It sort of degenerated into "Did not," "Did too," after that.

"*I'm* afraid of *you*?" I said. "*You're* the one who won't be seen in public with me. How do you think that makes *me* feel?"

"That's different."

"It is not."

"At least *I'm* not the one who's running away. *You* started it and then you ran away."

She had me dead right there, so I tried to change the subject. "Someone would have found out," I said.

"I thought you didn't care."

"I don't care."

"Neither do I."

"Yes, you do. You won't even walk down the street with me. You won't talk to me in class. You won't sit with me at the movies."

"That was before," she shouted.

"Before what?"

"Before I wanted to." She stood up and stormed across the room with her fists tucked up under her arms. Leaning against the wall, she looked out the front window and took a loud deep breath. After a while, she recrossed the room, poked at this chair that had a crooked golden slipcover, and sat down facing me.

"I want to," she said. "I want to learn how to drive. I want to go places. I want to grow up. It's not right to live like we're *stuck* in this time. My parents wouldn't have wanted that for me. I know it. They'd want me to grow up and make them proud, and just because they're not here doesn't mean I shouldn't do it."

Up until then, I'd always figured that I was the stronger of the two of us. But seeing how fierce she looked, and hearing how firm she sounded, made me think that I'd been wrong.

Or maybe I had just become wrong. Sometimes you don't know you feel something until you say it, and then, once it's said, you realize that you've felt it all along. So just as you finish talking, the words take on a different meaning. They aren't about some weird stirring inside you anymore, they're about a new conviction. It's like you're more when you finish than you were when you started. So maybe she'd just become stronger right there in front of me, sitting on that chair with the crooked golden slipcover.

I kept quiet after that, picking through my own memory. "I don't know what he would have wanted," I said at last.

"He would have wanted you to grow up," she said quietly.

"I used to think his whole life was an example and I was running after it, but I couldn't catch up," I said. "Now it seems like a warning and I can't get away."

"Not everything. Not his whole life."

"Yeah, sometimes it seems like his whole life was aimed at that accident, almost like we should have been able to see it coming, the way he was always the best and the coolest. He just thought he could do anything he wanted and make it come out right."

"But Bobby, what does that have to do with you?"

"I don't want to end up like that," I said. "I'm afraid that if I do what he did I'll end up like that. But if I don't do what he did, then it's like I'm forgetting all about him. But it's *not* like that because I think about him all the time and sometimes when I'm just lying there at night, I start remembering and I remember different stuff, stuff we did, and stuff we said, way back to when we were kids. All that time I was trying to be just like him, and I just lie there and miss him. I miss him real bad, but I don't want to end up like that."

She left the chair with the crooked golden slipcover and came over to sit beside me on the couch. Somewhere in there, when I started losing it, she put her arms around me and I leaned back against her.

"We're not gonna die," she said. "We're not gonna die."

I don't know why I wouldn't let her hold me. Sometimes you just feel too disgusting to deserve it, I guess. "You don't have to do this," I said, pushing her away. "I'm the one who ran away." I was standing in the hall, wiping my eyes, getting ready to leave.

"I don't understand you," she shouted. "One minute I think you're my best friend and the next minute you won't even let me talk to you."

Nothing much registered after she said "best friend." Her mouth kept moving, but my mind's ear, if there is such a thing, just kept hearing "best friend" over and over again. I hadn't had a best friend since the seventh grade when Kevin Mulhearn moved to Arizona. *Whoever thought your best friend could be a girl?* The thing of it was, it was true.

"What's so funny?" she said because I was grinning.

"It's not funny, it's nice. It's real nice."

"You are behaving like a child and you think that's nice?"

"No, the other part. The best friend part."

"Well, don't get a big head about it. You don't deserve it." She was holding a little bag from Paperback Booksmith. "Here," she said. "I got you a birthday present."

"You didn't have to."

"I wanted to, so just take it, okay? I hope you like it. It's about baseball, but it's about other stuff, too." The book was called *Baseball's Great Experiment* by Jules Tygiel and it was the story of how Jackie Robinson became the first black player in the major leagues. I knew some stuff about Robinson because my dad met him once in spring training in the sixties. He was a second baseman, too.

"Thanks," I said. "Thanks a lot. This is great." I told her about when Dad met him and about the 1955 World Series. "My mother's cousin Paulie in Brooklyn said it was like a piece of the city died when the Dodgers moved to Los Angeles," I said.

"How could people be that crazy about a game?" she asked.

We went back in, sat down on the couch, and drank tea. For the longest time, I told her how people could be that crazy about a game.

Diving

The first girl he ever liked was Maura Holmes and she cost me a tooth. I didn't know exactly what was happening at the time, because I was just going into eighth grade and missed the best gossip. All I noticed was that in the summer between his freshman and sophomore years my brother started having secrets. He spent a lot of time writing stuff he wouldn't let anybody read and going for walks by himself.

Later, when my mother told me why Billy was bumming out, the whole thing started to make sense. Maura Holmes had been to a couple of our Babe Ruth games that summer. She and her girl friends always talked to us when we went swimming at Ketchum Pool. I saw her at the door real early a couple of Sunday mornings when we were delivering our paper route.

In late September, she must have had a fit of bad taste,

because she dropped my brother for this hotshot senior named Dennis Kovach. He was high scorer on the basketball team and he played shortstop the season before for Coach Sherrill. He had a car.

For about the next two weeks my brother was about as lively as Reese Point after dark. Every day after school he'd go straight up to his room and do all his homework. I was afraid he might be on drugs or something.

Late one Saturday afternoon, when I'd come back from collecting my paper route, Mom said it might be a good idea if Billy and I played a little catch.

"He doesn't want to play catch," I said.

"He changed his mind," my mother said.

All I can figure is that she'd given him a big pep talk and told him to quit moping around. I'd bet any amount of money that she told him there were "lots of fish in the sea."

We went up to the field on the top of Trager Street and threw the ball around for a while, but there wasn't much point to it.

"Let's pitch and catch," Billy said just as it was starting to get dark.

Pitch and catch is pretty self-explanatory. One guy on the mound. One guy behind the plate. The catcher calls balls and strikes. You can play entire games if your knees hold out.

He pitched first. Usually, he liked to fool around with finesse pitches. Throw a curve ball, try a slider, even a knuckle ball. But that day he busted every pitch as hard as he could. Pretty soon my hand started aching. He was all over the place with his control. Walked the bases loaded. Went 3 and 2 with two outs. I don't think he even cared.

On the last pitch he took this huge windup and let the ball go from somewhere back near second base. It was coming in high, way out of the strike zone, and I straightened up to reach it. Maybe if I had been wearing one of those big pillow catcher's mitts I would have had a chance, but all I had on was my glove. The ball ripped across the laces and smacked me right in the mouth. I fell back, and grabbed at my face. There was blood on the ground and a piece of my tooth in the catcher's box.

Billy just stood out on the pitcher's mound with his head down and his hands on his knees. "You okay?" he called finally, but he had to know I wasn't.

Dr. Charnitski, our dentist, built the stump of the tooth up with some kind of white stuff. It looks pretty good, but when you run your tongue across it, it feels grainy.

That spring Billy beat out Dennis Kovach for starting shortstop.

12

My mother must have known how depressing it would be for her and me to be by ourselves the night of my birthday, so after Mass we drove over to Aunt Caroline's for dinner. Aunt Caroline is my godmother, which basically means that she is responsible for buying me presents. But if something ever happened to Mom and Dad, she'd be responsible for everything else, too. Annie Dunham lives with her godmother.

All through dinner I tried to imagine what it would be like living at Aunt Caroline's. She was nice enough, but I wasn't used to having little kids around, and Uncle Tim was one of those hearty lumberjack type of guys who kind of scared me.

After dinner Aunt Caroline unveiled this great-looking coconut marble cake. Her eight-year-old twins sang "Happy Birthday" to me. Mom gave me a new gray sports coat and a pair of blue pants to go with it. She said they were from Dad, too. Aunt Caroline gave me a white button-down and a burgundy tie. You could tell that they'd shopped together. My mother was always doing that. Every gift you got matched every other gift you got.

My best present was this new clock radio. It came from Don Becker, my godfather. He's a friend of Dad's. The old one hadn't been working too well since that one day when the whistle blew early.

Everybody tried real hard to make it a normal birthday, but the thing was that on normal birthdays, we never had to try. It was all pretty depressing, but I was proud of myself for not acting like I was depressed. Mostly, I couldn't wait to get back in bed with the Jackie Robinson book. Sometimes when you are reading something terrific you can just escape into this other world. Then when you're finished, it's like you've forgotten everything that made you sad.

We were back at the house watching TV when Mom left the room for a second and came back with this package wrapped in reindeer and holly. "I've had this a long time," she said, lifting it like something delicate was inside. "It was meant as a Christmas gift. I guess he got a good deal on it last summer."

Something from Dad, I thought, and started feeling all sentimental.

"I thought Christmas was too soon to give it to you," she said. "Maybe now is too soon, too. But I thought you should have it."

I grabbed the package and began running my finger under a seam in the wrap job. Opening gifts is a ritual in my family. We never just tear into something. I think we'd steam the paper off and save it if we could. "It's from Dad?" I said.

"Oh," my mother said. "No. It's from Billy."

I pulled back my hand, then lifted the package like it was a bomb and sat it on the coffee table. The whole thing was pretty Twilight Zony.

"You don't have to open it," my mother said.

"No, I want to. I'm just—it's just such a—a surprise."

"Do you want me to leave?"

I shook my head, leaned toward the table, and began playing with a piece of tape. Ever since that day when Annie told me the last thing that her parents said to her, I'd been thinking about the last thing that Billy said to me. It was "See you in a week, sport." So I tried to think back to the last time he'd said something important. All I could come up with was some of the long-past stuff that I've already told. Now, all of a sudden, he was going to say something. Unless it was just a tie. But the box was too big for a tie. Maybe a hat and some gloves—you could get those cheap in the summer.

I ran my finger up the side of the box. Underneath the wrapping I could make out these big script letters, but I couldn't tell what they said. Finally, I just flipped the damn thing over and tore off all the paper. After that, I wanted to cry.

It was a baseball glove. A Wally Backman, Mizuno baseball glove. I'd been crazy about it for almost a year. It had my favorite player's name in the pocket and I knew it fit me great because I'd tried it on up at the mall last spring.

103

I didn't take it out of the box right away. I just kept poking at it and feeling the leather and running my finger across the strands in the webbing. I even smelled it. There's nothing cooler than a baseball glove. You put one on and all of a sudden it's like you're a wizard. People might be showering you with rockets or pelting you with eggs, but it doesn't matter, because everything goes quiet inside the glove. Maybe a bat looks like a magic wand, but a glove feels like one.

I tried to stop feeling so good about it. Baseball was over for me. It was a whole painful world that I didn't have to deal with anymore. But people kept telling me I should play. Martinelli, Charley, even Annie had mentioned it. I figured my parents were happy enough for me to give it up, because that meant they could give it up, too. But here was the glove. From Billy, through Mom, to me. It sounded like a double play.

"Is it a good kind?" Mom asked.

"Yeah, it's a great kind."

"Are you going to try it on?"

"I'm pretty sure it fits."

"Well, you like it, then?"

I gave her what must have been a spooky-looking shrug.

"I'm sorry we couldn't give you a happier birthday," she said.

"You did," I said. "A lot," and kissed her good night.

I sat the box in the chair in my room and stared at it for a while. Then I decided to ignore it. In bed I reached for Annie's book, but baseball wasn't a good thing to take my mind off baseball. I felt like one of those guys in the cartoons who has an angel on one shoulder and a devil on the other. "Try it on." "Leave it in the box." I wanted to go with the angel, but which one was he?

Finally I decided to try it on. It was only a baseball glove. What kind of jerk loses sleep over a baseball glove?

So I stuck my hand in. The leather was even softer than I thought. The grain felt good against my palm, so I pounded in a pocket. The whole thing was bound together just tightly enough and the strap hugged my wrist. The only trouble was that the inspector's sticker was lodged in the middle finger. I kept digging at it until it fell on the bed.

I could see right away that it wasn't the inspector's sticker. Nobody else had that scratchy kind of handwriting. Nobody except Billy.

I opened the note real delicately, like I expected it to disintegrate in my hands. It was short. It was short even though I wanted it to be long. For some reason I thought it was going to be about life after death, or seeing the face of God or something like that. Instead, it was about baseball.

Dear Robert Thomas Michael,

This will be our last season to play together for a while, but I still want us to be teammates. Wear Mr. Wally when you're the best second baseman in the league and think about your poor freshman brother. Merry Christmas.

William Patrick Michael

105

After that all I did was sob. I just folded the glove against me like it was a teddy bear and kept on sobbing. When my mother knocked at the door I was rereading the note for about the twentieth time and never even heard her.

"What's the matter, honey?" she asked.

I held out the note and watched her eyes move over it. "Oh, Bobby," she said. "Oh, my God."

Diving

The stink of sulfur was on him every day when he came home. Mom used to make him undress in the cellar and throw his work clothes into the dry sink so she could wash them before bed. Sometimes, if he knew she wasn't home, he'd run through the house naked and jump into the shower. For the first couple of weeks he thought it was pretty cool working at the Ash. He and Dad would be at the breakfast table every morning wearing almost exactly the same kind of clothes. Hard hats, flannel shirts, dusty jeans, and those calf-high work boots with the steel toes.

I'd never known exactly what my father did at the Ash until Billy went to work there. Dad was a bagger. He wore goggles on his eyes and a mask on the rest of his face. Every day he sat on top of this huge machine that opened bags under a chute. When the bag was in place, he tripped a lever and the ash poured down into it. A different switch sealed the bag and pushed it onto a conveyor belt. A guy at the bottom threw it into a railroad car. Every forty-five minutes they changed places.

Dad and Billy worked in different parts of the plant, but nearly every day they met for lunch at the Whistle Inn across from the main gate. Billy came home full of stories about the machines and the raunchy jokes and who could drink the most boilermakers. He was only sixteen, but he got to act like an adult until quitting time. Then he'd peel off the clothes, scald himself in the shower, and turn into a kid again. I was pretty jealous.

One day, he was still in the bathroom about five minutes before we were due at Hobson Field for a Babe Ruth game. I thumped on the door, but he didn't answer, so I went in to find out what was up. The shower was still on, but I could hear him puking.

"Billy, are you all right?"

He puked again, but he didn't say anything.

"Are you okay? Are you sick or something?"

About thirty seconds later, he turned off the shower and slid back the curtain. His eyes weren't really focused. "Oh, man, I hate that place," he said.

I followed him into our bedroom, where he put on his number 7 Ryder Trust Company uniform. I was number 2.

"It stinks so bad in there you can hardly breathe half of the time," he said. "And it's hot. It's really hot all day. That's why those guys drink so much. They're sweating like mules all the time and breathing all that dust into their lungs."

He finished tying his sneakers and grabbed his spikes

from under the bed. "Dad doesn't have it too bad. His job is boring, but it isn't brutal. He knows Cy.

"But the other guys, Jesus. People are getting burned with hot water. They get their fingers stuck in those machines. And they all got that cough." He hacked softly. "Like they've been inhaling cigarettes since they were about five years old."

All the way to the field he talked about the noise and the smoke and the injuries. I thought it was pretty lucky that Dad knew Cy Ryder.

We were climbing the last hill when he said something that threw me off.

"We can't end up there," he said. "There's just no way you can let yourself end up there."

But I didn't see what he was worrying about. Everybody knew Billy was going into baseball. It did start me thinking about myself, though.

Dad was one of our coaches that year, and when we reached Hobson Field, he was standing on the first-base line hitting flies to the outfielders.

"Don't tell him I was puking," Billy said.

13

When Mom ungrounded me I started sneaking into the gym after school to watch the baseball team work out. The first couple of times I got away with it, but Friday, Sal Martinelli was late and I was standing right by the door when he walked in.

"Hi, Bobby," he said. "Kind of makes you ache for warm weather, doesn't it?"

I took a seat in the bleachers and watched them go through about fifteen minutes of calisthenics. Martinelli was right. There weren't too many upper classmen out for the team, mostly wiry little sophomores, kids built like me. When they broke into pairs to play some catch, Martinelli jogged over to see me. Along with him he brought Kenny Bibb.

Sal didn't know we knew each other, so he introduced

us, but then somebody came in needing to see him and he trotted away.

Kenny Bibb embarrassed the hell out of me the first time we met, but it was my own fault. Last year, when we were both freshmen, our schools sent us to this Youth Day conference in North Darden. The idea was to get a lot of kids who were on their student councils together and teach them God knew what. They broke us into groups and we spent most of the morning talking about "involvement" and "apathy" and "where the other guy is coming from."

Right before lunch we had what the group leader called a "self-expression task." We were supposed to make a poster of our "personal coat of arms." He told us to divide it into four sections and put a symbol in each one that stood for one of our goals or values.

I didn't figure anybody was going to get too personal, so I drew in a lot of obvious stuff: a glove for baseball, a book for being smart, a podium for public speaking, and a house for my family. I put the glove in especially because Bibb was in my group. I'd been reading about him in the sports pages since the seventh grade. He was a star in baseball, basketball, track, even Boys' Club floor hockey. I figured his shield would look like a calendar for a sporting goods store.

Once we got started, people talked about being popular, being a good athlete, earning money, all the typical high school stuff. It was as boring as the rest of the morning until Kenny's turn came. This cheerleader from Mount Wilson had just explained in ridiculous detail how the gold braid on her poster stood for good grooming.

"I can't draw very well," he said, holding up his poster. "But this, up here, is a lamb. That's for gentleness. And this is supposed to be a dove. You know, for peace.

"I don't know if you can really make this out, but this is a black hand holding a white hand. That stands for people getting along together.

"And this guy in the corner, this is Eddie Murphy. He stands for having a good sense of humor."

People actually clapped. It was like everybody realized how trite their own posters were and decided to laugh about it.

After that, I tried to jazz mine up a little. I said the book stood for learning the truth and the podium stood for telling it to the world, but it was still a pretty lame showing all in all.

When Martinelli told me Kenny was coming to our school, I felt sorry for him. He and his sister Beverly were the only black kids in the building. I figured if anybody my age could handle that, it was Kenny Bibb, but still, it had to be tough.

We weren't in any of the same classes, so I hadn't had a chance to ask him about it. I didn't think people would be nasty to him or anything, but maybe they just wouldn't know how to act.

"What's up?" he asked. "You coming out?"

"I don't think so."

"We could use you."

"Thanks. How you liking it here?"

"It's good, pretty good," he said. "It's school."

112

"Yeah, I'm still getting used to it, too. You hanging out with anybody?"

"Naah. You know, eat lunch with the guys in class. Practice with these guys here. Sometimes Sal gives me a ride home. He's a good guy."

Martinelli came jogging by and I figured Kenny would follow him, but he just stood there. "He wants you pretty bad," he said. "He thinks we'd be good together. You at second, me at short. Me leading off, you hitting behind me."

"Guess you guys have talked about it."

"Yeah," he said, chuckling. "I'm supposed to work on you."

"Sorry," I said. The idea of a sales pitch gave me the creeps. "I gotta go."

"Hey, Connely," he said, grabbing my arm. "I could use a friend on this team."

"I'm not ready to play," I said.

"What do you keep coming in here for?"

I didn't have an answer for that. "Look, my mom is going on a trip tonight," I said. "I gotta get home."

"You doing anything later?" he asked.

"Watching the house."

"I was gonna ask you if you wanted to come over to watch the Sixers."

I told him I couldn't and pushed through the door, but standing in the hallway I realized that I was being a jerk.

Swinging the door back open, I called his name. "Hey, I gotta stick around the house, but if you want to come over, we can pick up the Syracuse-Georgetown game on cable."

113

He said that would be great.

My mother was upstairs when I got home. "Your supper is in the oven," she called.

I was checking out the cubed steak and baked potato when Mom walked into the kitchen. She wore this light-blue dress that was almost the same shade as her eyes. Her hair was combed back and it looked longer than usual. She didn't look like my mother, or anybody else's mother for that matter. It was like she'd put on a more carefree personality and was walking around in it to see how it fit.

"Mom, you look really great," I said.

I hadn't seen her smile that way since Billy was alive. "Thank you," she said, and kissed me on the forehead. "I'm late. Are you sure you are going to be all right? What are you doing tonight?"

"I'm sure," I said. "One of my friends is coming over. We're gonna watch the basketball game." That sounded so normal I could hardly believe it was coming from me.

"That's nice," she said. She buttoned the long gray coat Dad bought her two Christmases ago and stood at the door for a minute, staring straight ahead. You'd have thought she was jumping out of a plane instead of stepping onto the porch.

"Tell Dad I can't wait to see him," I said.

She nodded like she didn't quite hear me and walked out the door with a smile on her face. Five seconds later she was back. "I'm so absentminded," she said, and snatched her keys off the table.

Kenny came over around seven. We ate about a bag and a half of Doritos watching the Orangemen and the Hoyas play to a 38–38 halftime tie. The second half was so frantic

114

we couldn't sit still. I dug out an old Nerf ball from under the couch and we started going one-on-one at a waste can we set on the coffee table. He was Larry Bird and I was Isaiah Thomas. Every now and then we'd stop and see what the college boys were doing.

We collapsed before they did, calling it quits and hauling out the Cokes just before Syracuse took it by a point in overtime.

"Who says this is a spectator sport?" Kenny said, wiping his forehead with his sleeve. He chugged about half his can of Coke.

"Sorry we don't have anything stronger," I said.

"Not for me."

"You don't drink?"

"Only on social occasions. Cotillions. Art gallery openings. Rumbles."

"Seriously."

"Only when I'm trying to fit in at beer parties. You?"

"I like to, I guess. Yeah, I do when I get the chance."

"Makes you fat," Kenny said. "But your old man is still pretty lean, so you can probably get away with it."

He had no way of knowing what he'd just said, and I tried with my reaction to keep it that way. "He's pretty trim," I said.

Kenny lobbed the Nerf ball at me and I snagged it in one hand.

"You gotta come out for this team, Connely," he said. "You're the Missing Link."

I pretended I was an ape with a baseball bat. "That's flattering," I said.

He started writing down lineups. "Here's us with you,"

115

he said, handing me one card. "Now here's us without you. A lot of guys would be happy because they could go back to playing their regular positions. It's like the domino theory."

I was pretty impressed that he'd managed to work evolution and foreign policy into his sales pitch, but I still didn't want to play. The problem wasn't baseball, it was all the stuff that baseball had come to stand for, and finally, I said so.

We were walking by that point. He lives about a mile and a half from me, but I know a shortcut through this empty lot behind the Super Saver. The path is a little spooky at night, so I was going to take him to the other side, then come back on the main roads.

"I know about your brother," Kenny said.

"Maybe that's not it anymore," I said. "Maybe I'm just scared."

Coming down the embankment behind the store, we saw a bunch of cars parked in the empty lot. A huge pack of kids milled around in the dark. You could hear voices buzzing. Every now and then somebody would swear or break out laughing.

"Looks like a pretty big party," I said.

"Check it out?" Kenny asked.

"Sure."

I used to love going to keg parties. Everybody seemed to like each other more when they were drinking. You made friends you never would have had. Some girl was always saying that some guy was "*sooo* funny" when he was drunk, like that was when your best self came out.

116

You learned a lot just by standing around getting shit-faced. It felt like you couldn't grow up without doing it.

A lot of the kids at this party were pretty hard-core. They kept hopping from foot to foot, blowing on their hands and gulping down beer. The kids around the fire turned around and around in the heat like they were bar-becuing themselves.

From the size of the crowd you could tell it was more than just a Reese Point party. I recognized kids I hadn't seen since we left Ryder. Kenny even knew a couple of guys from Consolidated, which was about eight miles away. He ran into an old classmate, so I stood on the edge of their conversation until I felt somebody tug on my sleeve.

"Hey, Bobby, hiya doin'?" It was Brian McHale. Brian was one of the only kids from Ryder who tried to keep in touch with me after we moved. We'd been on jayvee base-ball and student council together. I probably could have kept him as a friend except that's when I went into hiber-nation.

I said "Hi," and he started calling over some of the other guys I'd gone to school with. Somebody brought me a beer and pretty soon there were five or six of us in a little knot talking about who was going out with whom. They all wanted to know if Reese Point was as bad as everybody said.

I was sort of enjoying myself, but the conversation didn't go anywhere. It was just like Annie said, people were nice enough, but they didn't know what to say to

117

you. Besides, it was about eleven o'clock and a lot of the guys were already drunk.

After a while just about everybody drifted off. Brian and I were standing by the fire when he started getting nervous. "Guess you better find your friend," he said.

"No, it's okay. He's with some kids he knows from his old school."

Brain walked away, and when I didn't follow him, he came back and took me by the arm.

"What's going on?" I said.

"Come 'ere." He led me back through the crowd to the edge of the party. When Brian leaned over to whisper in my ear, I could smell beer and pepperoni pizza.

"Listen," he said. "Richie Munley is here. He just got his X rays back from his last surgery, man. They told him he can't play ball anymore."

Richie Munley. The last time I saw him he was running down a shot up the gap in the Tri-County championship game. My brother called him 'Lope, for antelope. I couldn't imagine him not being able to run.

"He's been shitfaced since about an hour after school," Brian said. "The guy is just looking for a fight. I'm not trying to get rid of you, man, I just think you should get the hell out of here."

I said thanks and pushed back into the crowd. I'd lost track of Kenny. The longer I looked for him, the itchier I got. Richie was a lot taller than me. He was skinny, but he was supposed to be strong. Maybe if it was just going to be a fight, I wouldn't have minded so much, but in some weird way it felt like my brother's honor would be at stake. People had been kicking that around long enough, but I didn't feel like much of a defender.

I'd just decided to head home when somebody grabbed my shoulder.

"Little B," Richie said. "Little Fuckin' B. Hey, how's your dead brother? Heh heh." His face was nearly the same shade as his fatigue jacket. His lower jaw seemed like it was barely connected to the rest of his head.

"Hey, Richie," I said, and tried to push past him.

"How the fuck you doin', Little B?" he said, punching me in the shoulder. It was playful enough, but it hurt.

"I'm doing okay, Richie." Where the hell was Kenny?

"Wanna know how I'm doing?" he asked. "I'm shitty. I'm real shitty." He started to spell it out, drumming me on the chest with each letter, but I knocked his hand away after the "i."

"Richie, I'm sorry about your leg and everything, but just cut it out, okay?"

"Aah. Poor Little B," he said. "Poor stupid Little B." He grabbed me by the shoulders and I thought he was going to push me down.

"Look, Richie, I don't want to fight," I said, but he wasn't listening.

"How come you're so stupid?" he said, sticking his face right into mine.

"Come on, cut it out," I said.

"Aw, cut it out," he said. "D'you get paid? You don't even know, do ya? *I* get paid."

I just kept walking backward, away from the rest of the

119

party, hoping he wouldn't start anything. We went out with the same girl once. I thought he was trying to tell me he got laid.

Richie followed me, laughing like a freaked-out animal. "So I don't give a fuck," he said. "I don't give a fuck if I play baseball, Little B. I'm taken care of. I-am-taken-care-of."

I grabbed a hold of his arms. "Richie, you're really drunk, okay? And you're talking crazy. I gotta go find my friend."

"*I'm* crazy?" he said, pushing me backward. "*I'm* crazy? You're the one who's fucked up, Little B. I'm the one that knows and you're the one that don't know."

"What are you talking about?"

He laughed like an animal again. "What happened," he said. He drew his hands apart and smashed his right fist into his left palm. "Pow." I could have done without the sound effects.

"I know what happened," I said. "I read the police reports."

"Oh yeah. Everything was *right* there in the police reports. Everything was *right* there. You stupid little shit. D'you ever hear of an accident where the driver dies but the guy riding shotgun gets out okay?"

"It could happen."

"It didn't happen," he said. "It didn't fuckin' happen."

"Richie, don't fool around about this."

"Poor Little B." He slapped me softly on the face. "Poor stupid Little B."

"Say what you're trying to say, Richie. Just say it."

He spit on the ground near my feet and turned back

120

toward the party. I called after him, but he kept walking away. I knew what he meant, but I wanted to hear the exact words right out of his stupid face. It didn't matter if he beat the shit out of me after he told me, just as long as he told me.

I got a running start and crashed into the back of his legs. He went down like a tree in a stiff breeze. In a second I climbed on his chest and pinned his arms with my knees. I thought he'd try to throw me off, but he just lay there looking sick.

"Who did it?" I said. "Who was driving?"

For a second I thought he was going to puke on himself. "It wasn't your brother," he said. "And it sure as shit wasn't me."

14

Running is all I remember. *Running* up the embankment. *Running* across the parking lot. *Running* down Railroad Avenue saying, "Faster. Faster. Faster." This is an old trick. If you race your body it quiets your mind. Like, "Sorry, I can't freak out right now, I'm *running.*"

Only it wasn't working.

Sooner or later Richie would realize what he had done. He'd tell Mark Ryder or *Cy* Ryder, or whoever was giving him the money. And then somebody would come looking for me. Taking no chances, I bolted down an alley and cut across a couple of yards. Hollow Hill Road was as quiet as usual, but I let myself in through the back door. In the kitchen I turned on the kerosene heater and pulled a chair over to sit in the warmth.

Mark Ryder was driving the car. Not Billy Connely. Mark Ryder.

I sat there waiting to feel good about that, but the good feeling never came. My brother wasn't driving. It wasn't his fault. But if it wasn't his fault, then something had happened that was just as terrible as the accident. And now it seemed like I was the only one who knew about it.

I pictured Mark Ryder's smirking face. It wasn't hard to understand why he'd *want* to do it, but it was hard to figure out how he'd be *able* to do it. His father must be in on it, but that didn't explain why the Tamble Ridge police blamed it on Billy.

I unlaced my hiking boots and tried to remember all the old newspaper coverage. Two mornings after the accident there had been a picture of Sheriff Ryder and a Tamble Ridge cop standing in front of the wreck. The sheriff looked like he'd slept in his clothes. "Sheriff to Lead Fatal Crash Probe" is what the headline said.

I didn't think that could be right, because I swear the Tamble Ridge police came to our house one night. But I remember that headline, too. It was right beneath the picture and I dreamed about that picture for two weeks.

So Sheriff Ryder must know about it, and some of his deputies too, and maybe the brother-in-law in the DA's office. It seemed like every important person around here was in on it. After that I got scared of being in the house alone.

The St. Joseph's brochure was underneath the telephone and I read the number with a flashlight. No one answered. I wanted to take off out into the streets again, just to calm myself down. "In. Out." I kept saying that with every breath. "In. Out."

Beneath the brochure was the bus schedule. There was

a two A.M. that stopped in White Birch Falls. It would put me at St. Joe's about five in the morning, but the sooner the better. I ran upstairs, packed my overnight case, ran back downstairs, and bounced through three or four rooms, full of not knowing what to do next.

Make a list, I thought. Make a list of everybody who needs to know. But shit, *every*body needed to know. Who can I tell? I called Charley first, half hoping he'd offer to drive me to White Birch Falls. "Come on, Cowboy, please be home," I said out loud, but his phone just kept on ringing. Something on the porch squeaked and I ducked behind the refrigerator. It squeaked again—and again—before I remembered the loose bolt on the mailbox. In. Out. In. Out.

I knew what was happening to me. I was on the verge of losing it. Losing it big time, the way I used to lose it right after Billy died. In. Out. Screaming, crying, smashing lamps, beating on walls, beating on people who pulled me off the walls. In. Out. Once I even gave my mother a bloody lip.

I loosened my death grip on the telephone long enough to dial Annie's number. Her line rang longer than usual. The voice on the other end wasn't hers. Here goes nothing, I thought.

"Hello, Mrs. McDonough. This is Bobby Connely," I said. "I need to talk to Annie. It's really important."

There was a long silence. "Whoever you are," she said, "I hope you've had your joke. And I hope you don't repeat it or we'll call the police." *Click.*

She must be downstairs, I thought, and flipped through

124

the phone book for the other number. This time her uncle answered.

"Is Annie at home?"

"Who's calling?"

"It's her friend Jane," I said in as high-pitched a voice as possible."

"Jane, it's twelve thirty at night," he said.

"It's very important."

"It will have to wait until the morning," he said.

"IT CAN'T WAIT," I screamed, but he'd already hung up.

Something about the dial tone spooked me. Suddenly talking to Annie seemed like it was a matter of life and death. So did getting out of the house. I snatched up my overnight bag, stuffed the bus ticket that Mom bought me into my pocket, and slipped out the back door. I didn't see a soul on my way to the McDonoughs', but once I got there, I realized that I didn't know where Annie's room was.

Through their front door I could see a glow that must have been the television. Annie and I both liked to stay up late and watch old movies, so I figured that's what she was doing. I thought of trying the phone again, but what if her aunt really did call the cops? I might disappear like one of those people in South America. Fuck it, I thought. I'm going up on the porch.

I stashed my bag behind her neighbor's hedge and walked as softly as a bandit across the front porch. She was sitting on the floor in a pink robe. Her arms were wrapped around her knees. I tapped real lightly on the

125

window and prayed she wasn't watching *Nightmare on Elm Street*. Nothing happened the first time, so I tapped a little louder.

Suddenly a howling exploded from the kitchen. It seemed like the whole house shook. *She has a dog, you jerk. How could you forget she has a dog?* I jumped the railing, threw myself over the hedges, and lay on the ground. Every light in the house was on in seconds. I thought of making a break for it, but there were faces in the windows. Cheever kept howling. I was spending entirely too much time lying in the snow.

It was a good five minutes before the dog calmed down and I felt brave enough to raise my head. All the lights were out, even the TV. I started to feel like I'd landed on another planet and pretty soon they'd hunt me down. Leaving her neighbor's yard, I saw another face in the window and flung myself back in the snow.

The door opened a crack. This thin voice said, "Bobby?"

"What?" I said it like she was disturbing me.

"What are you doing?"

"I have to tell you something. Meet me at the corner."

"I can't. It's almost one o'clock."

"It's real important."

When the door closed I sprinted out of her neighbor's yard and hid behind a phone pole. In a minute or two, her porch light flashed on. I heard a jingling noise. Coming down the sidewalk was Cheever, who turned out to be some kind of retriever, followed by Annie, who wore a ski jacket over her robe.

"Don't worry," she said as he sniffed up my leg. "He

126

won't hurt you. I needed some kind of excuse to get out of the house."

The dog was making me nervous. "This better be good," she said.

I nodded a lot, but suddenly it felt like I'd forgotten how to talk. "I saw Richie Munley tonight at a party," I said.

"Yeah?"

"He was drunk. He started saying stuff." The dog wouldn't leave me alone. I was starting to panic.

"Bobby, what? What did he say?"

"He said"—In. Out—"He said my brother wasn't driving the car."

She stepped back and stared at me.

"It was Mark Ryder."

"Bobby, that can't be right. The police said it was your brother. The newspapers said it was your brother. They didn't just make it up."

I grabbed her by the shoulders and the dog yipped at me. "But Richie was there," I said. "He was there." The dog growled and jumped on me. I let go and backed away.

"Keep him off me," I said.

"It's okay. He won't hurt you."

"Just keep him off me."

"Okay. Okay. Take it easy, huh?"

"I'm sorry. I'm— He said he got paid. Richie said he got paid. He kept telling me how I was stupid and didn't really know what happened and how he knew all about it and that's why he got paid."

"You said he was drunk," she said. "Maybe he was just trying to upset you."

"No, no, he meant it. Once he knew what he was doing

127

he tried to stop, but I made him tell me. I knocked him down. He said, 'It wasn't your brother and it sure as shit wasn't me.' "

"But why wouldn't anybody know?"

"People *do* know, Annie. People know but Mr. Ryder paid them off. And the cops can't do anything about it because it was his fat-ass brother who took care of the investigation. They just kept Mark's name completely out of it."

"This is scary," she said, looking around.

"I'm gonna go up to tell my mom and dad about it and see what they want to do."

"You know it's only going to be Richie Munley's word against the sheriff," she said. "Even if he says it again, nobody's going to believe him."

"They'll have to believe him," I said. "Once we get the truth out, they'll have to believe him."

She yanked on the dog's leash and we walked back up the block, where I dug my bag out from behind the neighbor's hedge. We were standing in front of her house when she said, "I'm glad it wasn't Billy."

"Thanks." That's what I'd been waiting to hear.

"Be really careful, okay?"

"I will."

She leaned across the dog and kissed me on the cheek. "Call me when you get back."

She walked up the steps to the house while I stood there feeling the kiss on my cheek. It was strictly an Aunt Caroline type of kiss, but we'd never even had one of those before. It seemed like the damnedest time to start.

128

Diving

In the late autumn of my freshman year a girl named Gretchen Larson broke up with Richie Munley to go out with me. I never thought Richie was that interested in her, so it didn't seem like a big deal. But my brother and his friends were amazed that any girl would drop a junior to go out with a freshman even though the girl was a freshman herself. Somehow this made us a cool couple and we started getting invited to junior class parties. I'd never been drunk indoors before.

One night Mark Ryder got the key to his parents' cottage at the lake and about ten of us went up there. We built a fire and drank some beer, and after a while couples started drifting off to the bedrooms. While I was making out with Gretchen I kept wondering if anybody was actually doing it, because it couldn't have been more than forty

129

degrees in there. Around midnight the girls all piled into their cars and headed home. We slept over.

Billy and I were stuffing more wood into the fireplace when Mark came back from the kitchen with a bottle of Jack Daniels. "Truth time," he said.

Everybody sat around in a circle. I had no idea what was happening.

Peter Jordan went first. Mark poured him a shot and Peter drank it. Nobody made a sound until he held out the glass and said, "Do it again." Then everybody went wild.

"First time with her, right?" Billy asked. Peter nodded. "Boom, titty, boom," Alan Rukauskaus said.

Billy took two shots and got pretty much the same response. So did Alan.

"My turn," Mark said. He poured himself one glass. Then another. When he gulped down the third one, everybody started cheering. "The sticky finger award," Peter said.

"Muff diver," my brother said. "Calling Dr. Muff Diver."

Mark poured himself another glass and everybody went, "Naaah?" He raised it to his lips and smiled like a monkey, then he handed it to me. "Do you know what we're doing?" he asked.

"Yeah, you're drinking one shot for every base you got to tonight," I said. The stuff about sticky finger is what gave it away.

"So drink up," he said. "Or didn't you get anywhere?"

I drank the first one so fast I didn't taste it until it was halfway down my throat. It burned in my stomach the way Ben-Gay burns when some asshole puts it in your jock.

"Another?" Ryder said.

I held out the glass.

"My brother the sex machine," Billy laughed.

"You're one of the boys," Mark said after I'd choked it down.

I never told anyone that the second one was wishful drinking. I spit it up before morning.

15

White Birch Falls isn't a whole lot to look at at five in the morning, but I wasn't a whole lot to look at by that point either. I drifted in and out of sleep on the bus and even dreamed about how I'd tell them. If I just blurted it out they'd be running around like somebody had set them on fire and I didn't want that. I wanted us to come out of there with a plan.

The sun still hadn't made much of a dent on the darkness when the bus pulled into the station. There was only me and the driver on board by that point and he said I could sleep in the back until eight fifteen. It seemed like I'd just closed my eyes when the engine roared. There was a new driver up front. "Time to get up," he called.

In the bathroom I washed my face and fished a clean shirt out of my overnight bag. The lobby was nothing more than a big closet with a ticket window and a couple of vending machines. I bought some Necco wafers and ate them for breakfast with a Dr Pepper. After that meal I would have killed for a toothbrush.

St. Joseph's is secluded even by White Birch Falls standards. It sits on a hill, three dirt-road intersections from County Road 73, which is a two-lane that's about a day's rain away from being a dirt road itself. It wasn't hard to see why this was a good place to get away from it all. The mountains were peaceful in a scary kind of way. The air was so crisp. Even the bare trees seemed beautiful.

Dad must love this, I thought. He'd grown up in the woods, at least until he was about ten or twelve. They used to raise hunting dogs and take them on marathon hikes through the hills above the river. That was before his father died and Grandma Connely moved her family down to Ryder.

I tried to picture my father as a kid and wondered if there was ever a time when he wasn't worrying about everybody around him. Mom said he was wild in high school, but I couldn't imagine that. He was always so conscious of what could go wrong. Even before everything did go wrong.

For a long time after Billy died, Dad pretended like everything would be all right and tried to get us to pretend along with him. It was like he was trying to remake the world for us. He read the self-help books and went to all the meetings and tried to make sure that we did the same.

Mom humored him and sewed a border on the quilt. I just got distant. There was never any evidence that things were getting better and finally he couldn't believe it anymore himself. I guess that's when he chucked it and started drinking. Sometimes self-destruction seems like the only honest statement you can make.

But now we had evidence.

They weren't expecting me so early at St. Joe's and they didn't mind saying so. But I was persistent with the little monk in the brown robe who opened the door. He led me into this small antiseptic-looking office and began explaining the program. I couldn't see both my parents at once, he said, just my father. I tried to tell him that this was an emergency, but he said Dad and I needed to get "reacquainted." That word reminded me of what Annie said about how easily things get lost.

After he left the room I sat there for about twenty minutes looking through all these Catholic magazines. The monk was beaming when he came back and gave me directions to "the foot of the pond trail," where he said Dad would be waiting.

All the way out there my head was filled with "Dad, I have something to tell you." No. "Dad, I found out something pretty important last night." Better. But as soon as I saw him I forgot everything. He was standing in a clearing wearing an old pair of gray work pants, a blue woolen sweater, his AC jacket, and a corduroy Pirates hat. I felt like I was seeing him in an old home movie. He didn't just *look* younger, he looked like he'd *become* younger.

I didn't know how to act. *He* seemed healthy, but the moment seemed fragile. The hug we had was awkward because I didn't really know if I should squeeze him or not.

"I missed you," I said.

"I missed you, too, son." He started down a dirt road

covered with a thin crust of ice and lined with bare trees and I fell in next to him.

"How's Mom?" I asked, not wanting to dive right in.

"She's fine. We had a nice quiet dinner last night and a nice talk. You're here early," he said.

"Yeah, I have something really important I wanted to talk to you about. . . ."

"I have some pretty important things to tell you about too," he said. That's when he started into how sorry he was about what had happened the night before he left. Things were going to be different, he said. We were going to get on with our lives. I kept saying, "Good," and "Sure," and "That's great," because things *were* going to be different, just as soon as I told him about Billy.

He loved Mom very much, he said. She was a strong woman. By that point I couldn't hold it in anymore.

"Dad, I saw Richie Munley last night."

"Where was he?"

"We ran into him when I was walking one of my friends home."

"He and Billy were inseparable," he said, then looked a little angry with himself. Inseparable wasn't the right word.

"That's what he was talking about," I said. "He was talking about Billy."

Dad quit looking at the far shore of the pond and looked at me.

"Richie said that the night of the accident, Billy wasn't driving the car."

My father stopped walking.

"He wasn't driving. Mark Ryder was driving. Richie

135

got paid not to say anything about it, and Mr. Ryder and his brother took care of it after that."

Dad didn't say a word. I stood there waiting for him to sort it out, but he didn't look confused, or enraged, or overcome. He just looked sick.

"Dad, I can't believe it. *He wasn't driving.*"

Maybe it was the shadows, but I could see all the shine wearing off his old home-movie self. He looked like he looked three weeks ago. I could feel him searching through this new I-am-an-alcoholic vocabulary for the right thing to say.

"Everything is going to be so different now," I said, trying to help him.

"I know," my father answered.

"What?"

"I know."

"You know about Billy?"

He nodded.

"You *always* knew?"

He nodded again.

I have never passed out, but now I think I know what it would feel like. My knees got weak, my stomach turned, I felt like I was losing my balance. For a second everything went black, but when the blackness went away, I was still standing there. "Daaad?"

He started talking fast and took a step toward me. "Bobby, try to understand what we were faced with."

I backed away. "Does Mom know too?"

"We both know," he said. "I have a friend who works with the police in Tamble Ridge. They came to the house one night."

I didn't try to get any information after that, I just wanted to say the worst things possible. "Are *you* getting paid?"

"Bobby, try to understand. . . ."

"Understand what?"

"There was just nothing we could do."

"You could have told the truth."

"I did the best I could for us," he said.

"That's a laugh."

"They had the sheriff, son. They had the boys who were still alive. All I knew was . . ."

"They had your job," I shouted at him. "Your new job."

"Yes, they had my job," he snapped, and I was glad he still had some pride left for me to hurt. "If we fought this I would have been out of work. We're not going to get you through college on what your mother makes selling shoes."

"I don't give a flying fuck about college," I said. "You could have done something else. You could have tried."

"I did try," he said.

"Like hell you did."

He stood there looking like a sap and I stood there hating him for looking that way.

"Who else knows?"

"The McDonoughs," he said. "They are the aunt and uncle of that Dunham girl. Cy is taking care of them so they'll have enough money to raise her. A lot of what was decided was decided for the children's sake."

"Thanks," I said. "Thanks a lot. Couldn't you at least have told me?"

"Your mother wanted to tell you," he said. "We probably would have someday, when you were older. We would have told you when you were ready to leave. Bobby, there's nothing we can do about it. We can't let it . . ."

"There's nothing *you* can do," I said. "There's nothing *you* can do."

He called my name, but I was running back the way we'd come. I remember wondering if I'd ever see him again and where I was going to live now. "He is not your father," I said to myself. I felt like screaming it. Maybe it would have ripped the guy's guts out, but I didn't care. Right then I was just glad to know that there were ways of getting even.

16

I was going to run away.

My plan was to get back on the bus and ride it until they threw me off. When we hit the Ryder–Reese Point station I stood in the rest room for about fifteen minutes smelling the piss and the disinfectant until the bus pulled out again.

Once, when the Cowboy used to take the bus back and forth to school every weekend, he saw himself sitting in the same seat of what looked like the same bus, heading in the opposite direction. "Purgatory must be one long bus ride," he said.

That's the way most people look at it. You've said good-bye to everybody at one end of your trip, but you're hours away from everybody at the other. So while you're on the bus, it's like you're nowhere at all. That was okay with me, because I didn't have any place I wanted to be.

When the bus turned off the highway I slipped back into

the rest room. "Station stop is Darden," the driver called. "Termination point of this route. This is as far as she goes, folks."

That had to be a mistake. I waited until the bus emptied out. About five minutes later, somebody tapped on the door. "Hey, you," the driver said. "She needs repairs. We're loading another bus at platform two. *If* you got a ticket."

"I thought this route went all the way to Key West," I said, squatting down so it would sound like I really was using the toilet.

"The route does, but the bus don't. Your connection's at platform two."

"I'll be out in a minute," I said.

This wasn't looking good. I tried to board the other bus, but the driver asked to see my ticket. It is pretty lame to decide you're running away from home and then wind up stranded at the end of a three-dollar bus ride. There was nothing *runaway* about it. I could have been there to shop, or visit Aunt Gracie and Uncle Jimmy, or look at the campus.

The lobby was filled with college kids dragging duffel bags behind them. They made me feel younger than I do in a roomful of adults. I'd never actually been to the campus, even though it was the last place where Billy was alive. I got to thinking that visiting DSU might be like going to visit him. I'd never been to the grave site. I didn't even like driving through our old neighborhood. This would be sort of like paying my respects, now that I had some respects to pay.

The campus sits on a hilltop on the southeast side of

140

town. The bus ride from the terminal starts in a weary-looking neighborhood that's mostly empty lots filled with waist-high weeds. But the scenery brightens up a little as you climb the hill.

University Street is lined with old Victorian houses. They looked so cozy that I tried to imagine what it would be like to live in one. I figured there'd be fathers in fat chairs reading to their kids and old ladies baking cookies in the kitchen. I wanted to get off the bus, walk into one of those houses, and have everybody say hello to me, just like I belonged there. But I couldn't do that, so I sat on the bus and hated the people who could.

A quarter mile from the university the homes began to look a lot more ramshackle. The streets were packed with students. Most of the kids wore down parkas and they looked like the Michelin Man in blue jeans. But even in the cold they moved along real easily, like they owned the place. I guess, in a way, they did. It was a city of kids.

I tried to imagine Billy picking his way across the quad. The buildings closest to me were the newest, all brick and glass with these huge windows and weird silver sculptures out front. They had to teach engineering in there, I thought, or architecture. That's where his classes would have been.

Some of the students didn't look much more grown up than I do, which was kind of cool and kind of scary. It made me wonder what I would look like when I was their age, and where I'd be. *"A lot of what was decided was decided for the children's sake,"* my father said.

I rode to the south end of campus because I was afraid to get off the bus. Finally, I climbed down outside the

141

basketball arena, which I recognized from TV. There were enormous practice fields on two of the other corners and a long, low office building on the third. I drifted across to one of the fields where a bunch of guys in heavy sweats were running laps.

It took a while before I made out the "DSU Baseball" written in block letters on their shirts. To me the guys seemed huge. They were running in a pack the way you see them in Army commercials.

What happened next was that I spaced out a little and lost track of time. For some reason I was thinking that my brother would have been at DSU this year instead of next. I started to think that he would have been running with those guys, right that second. Thinking that he would have been there made it seem like he was.

I know this is weird, but I started talking to him. I asked if he was okay and he said yeah. I asked if it hurt much and he said no. I started to tell him what was happening at home, but he said he already knew about it. "Everybody is going to know the truth, now," I told him, but he didn't seem to care. He just said to be good to Mom and Dad. That kind of threw me because I figured he'd be like one of those old movie ghosts who kept roaming the earth until somebody cleared his name.

"Thanks for the glove," I said. I think by that point I was talking out loud, and I lost him. After it was over I didn't really believe it had happened, but it still felt like it had.

I walked along the fence a ways until I noticed this knotty little guy leaning against the backstop in the far corner of the field. "That's Blackie Sherwood," I said to myself. "That's Blackie Sherwood."

In our part of the world Blackie is a pretty big deal. He'd been a third baseman in the sixties, kicking around the minors for most of his career. One season he hit .253 for the Astros, back when they were still the Colt .45s, but that was the best he ever did. He didn't really get famous until after he retired in sixty-eight and began coaching in the instructional leagues. For six years he took classes part-time at the University of South Florida. It surprised the shit out of people when he got his degree. After graduation, he managed one season in the Texas League, but then the DSU job opened up.

Blackie pretty much took their search committee by storm. He told a few baseball stories to get their attention, then he said that he knew the value of an education because his college experience had changed his whole life. They cancelled the rest of the interviews after that.

Blackie has been at DSU twelve seasons now. He's made the College World Series ten times and the finals twice. He's never won the damn thing, but that just adds to his popularity. Most of the great baseball schools are down south, so people have this image of Blackie battling the elements, like he's living in a Greek myth or something.

Billy had been more excited about the chance to play for this guy than he had been about the chances of winning a scholarship. I wanted Blackie to think the right things about my brother, so, watching him talk to his team, I decided to tell him what had really happened. When the

143

huddle broke up, his guys bolted for the showers and Blackie headed for his office. I ran to catch up.

Billy's death was kind of a touchy subject around DSU. Blackie and the school had taken a lot of heat for the accident because the kids were under their supervision most of the time. But Blackie defused the situation by saying it was his responsibility and that next year he'd have an earlier curfew and more dorm monitors. He promised to speak personally with every tavern owner in that part of the county if that was what it took. Since no one really blamed him to begin with, that was more or less the end of it.

"Hello, Mr. Sherwood?" I said when I caught up with him.

"Hello," he said, grinning his small-mouthed grin. "What can I do for you?"

"I'm Billy Connely's brother," I said. "I'm Bobby."

That threw him a little, but he tried not to let it show. "What brings you to Darden?" he asked.

"Just looking at the campus," I said.

"You think you'd like to come to school here?"

"I don't know," I said. "It's nice, though. It's like a town full of kids."

He laughed at that. "I guess it is," he said. "Did you come down with your folks?"

"No." He looked at me like I was supposed to say something more. "I took the bus."

We pushed through the doors that led into the athletic department offices and he steered us down a long hallway.

"How are you enjoying Ryder High?" he asked.

"We're in Reese Point now."

144

"That's right. I guess I heard about that." He drew a deep breath and I knew he was going to say something about Billy. "You know we were very sorry around here about what happened to your brother."

"I know it caused a lot of trouble," I said.

"He was a good boy. Don't let anybody tell you otherwise."

"That's what I wanted to tell you about," I said. "We just found out that he wasn't driving the car."

"Well, I guess that's a comfort of a kind, isn't it?"

"Mark Ryder was driving."

"It was such a tragedy for everyone involved," he said. "That poor McDonough girl."

"He didn't kill her parents," I said.

"It must help to know that."

I couldn't believe it. He was hearing everything I said, but it was like it didn't make any difference to him. "It's a big difference," I said.

At his door, he asked me if I wanted to come in, but I said no. "Well, thanks for stopping by," he said. He knew I was pissed off at him. "Give my best to your parents."

"Yeah. Well, 'bye."

When I was halfway up the hall he called, "Have a good season." It was all I could do to keep from screaming, "Go fuck yourself."

A tragedy for everyone involved. Mark Ryder was cruising around in exactly the same kind of car. How come it was important when my brother was guilty, but it didn't matter now that he was innocent?

17

It was dark by the time I got back to the station. The next bus for Reese Point left at nine. That gave me about an hour and a half to kill. I bought some cheese and crackers and a can of Coke. After dinner I tried to call Annie, but that was the night of her driving lesson. Her aunt answered and I hung up. On one of those little six-inch pay TVs, I watched the evening news. When it was over I saw that Vanna White was up to something slinky on *Wheel of Fortune*, so I stuck in another quarter.

A bus station is a pretty lousy place to hang around because nobody really wants to be there. Everybody wishes they were old enough to drive or rich enough to own a car. They're pissed at themselves because that isn't the case, and they aren't too thrilled with you, either. I tried Annie again at eight and this time she was home.

"Hi, it's me," I said. "I'm in Darden."

"What are you doing there?"

"I tried to run away, but I got thrown off the bus."

"Bobby, what happened?"

"They knew about Billy. Your aunt and uncle know, too."

"How?"

I laid the whole story out for her, right down to Dad saying how much of it was done for the kids' sakes.

"Oh my God," she kept saying. "Oh my God. I wish I could . . ."

By the time I finished she was incredibly pissed off and I have to admit it was good to hear somebody else feel that way.

"How could they not *tell* me?" she said. "God, I wish I could . . . I don't want that money. I'm telling them I don't want that money."

"It doesn't matter," I said. "Nobody cares. I went to see Blackie Sherwood while I was down here. The baseball coach. I told him Billy wasn't driving and he acted like it didn't even matter. He just said it was a *tragedy* for everybody involved. Like the Ryders are really suffering, right?"

"Are you going to come home now?"

"I guess so. I don't know where else to go."

"Come home," she said. "I have to baby-sit at the Levinskis'. Do you know where it is?"

"Yeah."

"I really need to see you."

"Okay, if I can."

"At least call. They'll be out until real late, two or three or something."

The ride home took forever. I was really ticked off and really hungry. I figured that at least I owed myself a decent meal, so when the bus hit the station I headed for Lucy's.

Lucy's is a cross between a greasy spoon and a family diner. It sits right on the Reese Point–Ryder line. The neighborhood is a little too funky for most people, but just by the force of her personality Lucy has made the place seem semirespectable. She serves huge portions of everything, which also helps.

I slid into a booth near the door and ordered an open-faced turkey sandwich with mashed potatoes and gravy. It is one of those meals that sits in your stomach through entire phases of the moon. I had it about halfway down when the door swung open and in walked Mark Ryder, with whoever it is that's following him around these days.

My first impulse was to lay four bucks on the table and bolt, but I'd spent the whole day running from one place to another and I just didn't feel up to it. When he finally caught my eye I'd been sitting there a good ten minutes, thinking about everything that had happened to us since Billy died, and how much of it wouldn't have happened if people knew the truth. I knew the truth, but it seemed as though I wasn't going to be able to do anything about it. I thought the least I could do was make him feel a little uncomfortable about that.

When one of his friends went to the bathroom and the other got up to follow some girl, I paid my check and walked over to Mark's table. He was joking with a guy at the next booth, so he didn't see me right away. I just stood there playing with the salt shaker until he turned around.

"Hi, Bobby," he said, acting real cool.

"Hi." For another little while I kept on playing with the salt shaker. I could tell I was making him nervous.

"You want something?" he asked.

"I know what happened," I said.

"What are you talking about?"

"You were driving." I butted my fist into the palm of my hand, just the way Richie Munley had.

"You're crazy."

"Maybe. But I know what I know and I'm no good at keeping secrets."

"That's bluff," he said. "Your old man will be out on his ass."

His friends came drifting back, so I kind of sauntered out the door feeling pretty proud of myself.

Maybe twenty yards from the diner I heard someone behind me. Before I could turn around he wrapped one arm around my neck and pulled my right hand way up behind my back. His face was close to my ear.

"I'm not fooling," he said. "You better watch what you say or you'll be sorry. You hear me?"

"You'll be sorry, too," I said.

"Your brother's dead, man. I'm not gonna let this shit ruin me. You understand?"

He twisted my arm until I thought it would break. It was getting hard to breathe.

"Understand?"

"Yeah."

"Sure?"

"Yeah."

"Positive?"

"I said yeah."

I couldn't really tell what happened behind me after that. Suddenly we went spinning toward the ground, me, Ryder, and whoever'd jumped him. I landed hard, right on top of him, and he lost his grip. When I rolled away, there was the Cowboy.

He jumped on Mark's back and twisted one of his arms, the way Mark had twisted mine. With his other forearm Charley pushed Mark's face down into the pavement.

"You know I wouldn't mind wearing a little skin off your nose," the Cowboy said. "But I'd hate to have to do anything to the prize pitching arm."

"You're in big trouble," Ryder said.

"Suppose I am," Charley said. "How long do you think it's going to take me to come looking for you when my trouble's over?" He gave Mark's arm a quick jerk.

"Now my friend and I are going over to get in my car," Charley said. "I don't want to see you move until I'm inside with my stereo on. That way, if you say something stupid, I won't hear it. And if I don't hear it, I won't have to come back here and kick the living shit out of you. You got it?"

The Biscayne was right across the street. I hopped inside in about two seconds flat, but Charley took his time. Mark stayed on the ground until he heard the door close.

"That's the gladdest I've ever been to see you," I said.

"What the hell was going on?" he said, revving the engine.

"He didn't like something I said."

"BC, you feel like telling me what the hell happened or do you want me to go back there and feed you to him?"

150

"It was about my brother," I said.

"Yeah?"

"He wasn't driving the car that night. Mark was."

All of a sudden, Charley swung the Biscayne into a parking lot and cut the engine. "Tell it," he said.

I ran it all back without much enthusiasm because I hated the story already. "But I guess that there's nothing we can do," I said.

"Whaddaya mean? You gotta do *something.*"

"My dad won't."

"BC, it's not just about you and your family. The sheriff is in this and the DA. It's about the whole county. You don't know who else this kind of shit happens to."

He didn't say anything else, but all the way to the Levinskis' I could tell he was thinking up a plan. Part of me was rooting for him because I knew he was right. But part of me wanted to smash him in the face. He had no idea what this had done to my family. What it might still do.

18

We were sitting on this ugly old couch in the Levinskis' living room. The three-year-old had been in bed for hours. The six-year-old had just gone to sleep. I told Annie what happened down in front of Lucy's and she made me stand in the middle of the living room waving my left arm in circles and rolling my neck. She said that's what they did at the hospital where she used to volunteer, to see if there was any muscle damage. I told her I was fine, but she kept squeezing my shoulder and the base of my neck.

"Does that hurt?"

"No, I'm weird that way. Pinch me and it tickles."

"Sorry. Does this feel better?"

She was standing behind me, massaging my neck with her fingertips. "Mmmm. What do you think?" I said.

"I hope he doesn't come after you again," she said.

I gave her this bored sigh, to make it seem like I wasn't

afraid of him. She kneaded my muscles a little harder. "What do you think we should do now?" she asked.

"Watch TV."

"You're being a jerk," she sang.

"You don't like TV?"

"You know what I mean." She swatted me softly on the side of the head.

"Nothing," I said. "We shouldn't do anything now."

"Bobby, you have to."

"Why? Nobody cares. It's never going to come out and if it does come out it's just going to screw everything up. My stupid father would lose his stupid job, and your aunt and uncle would get cut off in about two seconds flat. I'll end up at the Ash *working* for the asshole and you'll be dishing out goddamn scalloped potatoes at Lucy's."

She stopped the massage and sat down on the couch with her arms folded across her chest.

"So we don't need to do anything now, okay?"

"I hate that we get that money," she said. "I hate it."

"You have it coming to you."

"I don't want it," she snapped. "It makes me feel like somebody owns me. It makes me feel like a whore."

"Hey! It's just the same thing as if you sued them."

"But we don't get it because Mom and Dad are dead. We get it because we don't say anything. We get paid to lie."

"So do we."

"I hate that."

"But it's not our fault."

"It *feels* like it is."

She wasn't appreciating my attitude about all this and

was probably on the verge of saying so, when the tea kettle whistled. I guess from the kitchen I didn't seem so despicable, because the softness came back into her voice. "You must be exhausted," she called. "Why don't you lie down on the couch for a while. You don't have to sit around here like it's a museum, you know."

I unlaced my hiking boots and swung my feet up on the couch. Hunting dogs chased ducks across the fabric. The armrests were big flat slabs of pine. I guess the idea was to feel like you were camping out even when you were at home.

She came in with the mugs on a little silver tray. Two streams of steam rose around her face. "A little bit of sugar, right?" she asked. I didn't answer.

When you are around a person for a long time, you put them into a category and sometimes you forget what you thought about them in the first place. In the first place, Annie Dunham had been one of the prettiest girls in the Ryder freshman class. When she passed you in the hall, one of your friends would say, "How'd you like to get a piece of that?" and everybody would go, "Yahoo."

I always liked the way she moved. It seemed as though she wouldn't leave tracks. Of course, I also liked what she moved, which was shaped to make you ache from thinking about it. All the guys wished that she'd gone out for cheerleading so we could have seen her in a short skirt.

I had two classes with Annie last year. Sometimes I'd look across the room at her and wonder why it seemed like there was hardly any white in her eyes. The brown there

154

glowed like a fire going out. I always thought she was keeping a secret.

While the other girls in our class charged into being grown-ups, it seemed like Annie hung back half a step. She seemed to know that something hard was ahead, even before the hard thing presented itself. Not that I said any of this to her. She was out of my league.

"Right?" she said again.

"Yeah. Yes, sugar."

She looked at me as if to say "What's gotten into you?" which was the question I was just asking myself. In the couple of weeks that I'd known her, I stopped thinking about the way she moved and tried not to look at her breasts when she arched her back. What was going on between us had boundaries. Everything we said or did had to do with the accident. I didn't think of her as a girl, I just thought of her as Annie, and I figured she was doing the same with me. The trouble was that without even knowing it, I'd started to look at her differently.

She bent over the tray and spooned sugar into the tea. The steam kept rising. I tried to look at a magazine.

"I told my uncle that I knew," she said.

"What did he say?"

"He's such a jerk. He said, 'That doesn't need to concern us.'

"I told him about you, too. I told him that you were the one who found out the truth and that we were—that you were my friend. He said your brother was still part of it."

"You're right, he's a jerk," I said.

She seemed hurt when she handed me the tea. Her eyes

155

darted around the room, like they were looking for some-place to hide. I'd known right along what kind of asshole I was being, but suddenly I felt really sorry for it. Her eyes settled on the rug.

"I used to wonder what would be the best thing that could happen for you and I thought that this would be it," she said, "that you would find out that Billy wasn't driving and it would really help you.

"Then I tried to think of what would be the best thing for me. I knew there couldn't be a best thing, not like that. Your brother will always be connected with it for me, Bobby. He was still drunk. He was still there."

I felt like I'd fallen through the floor and was looking up at her from the basement. For the last twenty-four hours I'd been running around with the idea that my brother was innocent. Now she was saying it wasn't true. Billy wasn't innocent. Maybe he was less guilty, but that seemed a lot less important, or at least a lot less clear. The thing was, I knew she was right. He *was* still drunk. He *was* still there. Being in the accident didn't undo any of the good he'd ever done, but not driving the car didn't make him a saint, either.

"But that's not the important thing," she said.

"It is the important thing."

"Not to me. I don't think of you in terms of your brother anymore," she said. "I just think of you as—you."

Her eyes were gleaming, but she didn't cry. My eyes were probably gleaming, too. For three or four seconds we sat completely still, looking at each other like we'd never seen another human being before.

156

It wasn't the way it is sometimes, when maybe you can kiss the girl and maybe you can't, and if you don't kiss her now, maybe you'll kiss her later, or maybe you won't, but all you will have missed out on is a kiss. It was more like knowing that just then, you were closer to that person than you ever thought you'd be, and that if you didn't kiss her, and kiss her soon, there'd never be another chance, and your life would be different because of it. The difference would begin as soon as she realized that you weren't going to kiss her, and maybe, however long it took, the death of it would start right there.

I didn't want us to die, so I kissed her.

It was a real shy kiss at first, like a swimmer wading into the ocean. But the water was warm, and the deeper we swam, the warmer it got. It was so warm that it never seemed like we had to do anything but kiss and kiss again and keep on kissing.

For a long time after that, we held each other and didn't say a word. She fell asleep with her head on my shoulder, then I fell asleep, too.

The next thing I heard was a car door slamming and Annie saying, "Oh my God. Bobby, they're home. It's two thirty. Oh, my God."

She threw my coat at me, swooped up the tea tray, and ran into the kitchen. "The front door," she said. "When they come in the side door, you go out the front."

I scooped up my boots and followed her. "Bobby, get . . ."

We kissed one more time before she broke away from me. "Now get out of here," she said.

I ran through the living room hauling on my coat. The

157

second that the Levinskis opened one door, I sneaked out the other. At the edge of their front yard, I started running. It was about two blocks before I realized that my boots were in my hands.

Diving

"I know he's your friend," I said one night driving back from this extremely half-assed fishing trip, "but it seems like Mark can be kind of . . ."

"Kind of a jerk?" Billy said. "That's because he *is* kind of a jerk."

"How come you hang out with him, then?"

"He's a good time."

That didn't seem like much of an answer, but I didn't say so.

"He's going to be a pretty big guy around here someday."

"Great."

"He'll probably be just like his father."

"I thought you hated his father."

"He sucks. Even when he's being nice to you he's always letting you know it. Like he could stop being nice to you any minute and then you'd be screwed."

"So if Mark is going to be like that . . ."

"I just like Mark now," he said. "I'm not going to be around then."

"Do you think that's what Dad thought?" I was just thinking out loud, but Billy got pissed.

"I'm not Dad," he snapped. "Baseball's just a way to get somewhere."

He said that a lot, but I never knew if he meant it. "I wish you wouldn't always talk about leaving," I said.

"That's a long time from now."

I turned on the radio, but there was nothing but static.

"I guess I figure if I hang around enough with him now," he said, "then I'll always remember that I don't want to have to be hanging around with him later."

19

After that a couple of weeks passed and all there is to say about it is that a couple of weeks passed. My dad came home, Annie flunked her driving test for forgetting to signal when she pulled out after a K-turn, and I started working out with the Reese Point baseball team.

I didn't actually decide to go out for baseball, I just woke up the morning after Annie and I kissed and knew that I was going to do it. My mother came home from St. Joseph's early that night and I asked her if it was okay. We ended up talking about baseball instead of about what Richie Munley told me. When she tried to bring it up, I said I understood what they had to do. That was pretty much the end of it.

After dinner I called Kenny to tell him I was coming out and he started doing this brutal Howard Cosell impersonation: "And so, the Keystone tandem is set. Bob

Connely, the sure-handed second baseman. Ken Bibb, the rangy shortstop. Tri-County League opponents may well rue the day young Connely made his momentous decision."

"That's the worst Cosell I've ever heard," I said.

"No way. The worst Cosell *is* Cosell."

In the second week of March, winter gave us a break. Sal Martinelli had us out in the soggy grass taking infield and batting practice for the first time. Later that week my dad started showing up. He always left before practice was over. I couldn't tell if he didn't want to be seen with me, or if he thought I didn't want to be seen with him.

This isn't a great thing to admit, but I wasn't paying too much attention to my father at that point. Playing with Kenny was just like Sal said it would be. He was always aware of where everyone on the diamond was and what they were doing. The rest of the guys began to look up to him as much for his concern as for his ability.

Playing for Sal was pretty great, too. He wasn't a bossy, military type like Sherrill. He liked joking around with us. The scouting report he'd given me on the team was pretty accurate. We were young and inexperienced, but we had a chance to be good. Danny Ratchford was our best pitcher, and we had a chance to win any game he started.

Ratch could hit a little, too. When he wasn't pitching he swapped positions with Tommy Paultz. We called Tommy, Beaner or Beanpole, because of the way he was built. His body was the exact opposite of Johnny Dukus's. The Duker was our catcher. He went about five foot six, 185 pounds. He wasn't too fast, but he was good behind the plate, and when he caught up with a fastball he could really launch it.

Third base was kind of a weak spot because Eddie Ciccone was kind of a weak player. But the outfielders covered a lot of ground and Pat Carr, who played left, was murder on right-handed pitchers.

We didn't figure to score a lot of runs, but unless everybody hit the ball right at Ciccone, we didn't figure to give too many away either.

After the first week of practice I started to feel pretty comfortable, so the next Monday, I dug out Billy's book and brought it to school. At first I thought I'd only show it to Kenny. He was smart, fast, and aggressive. With Billy's tips about the pitchers' pick-off moves, he could steal four or five bases a game.

"Every pitcher in the league?" Kenny said, leafing through it.

"Every one."

"This is outrageous," he said. "You have to show this to Sal."

I am a little shy about showing Billy's secrets to people, but Sal had been brooding up a storm all day and I thought maybe he could use a little cheering up. When I came off the field to take batting practice he was in the dugout. "I wanna see you bunting today," he snapped.

I was going to ask what was wrong, but it seemed like that might just tick him off even further. "I have something to show you," I said, digging the book out of my duffel bag. "But you have to swear you'll never talk about it with anybody."

163

"On my children," he said. Sal doesn't have any kids, but I handed him the book anyway. Pretty soon his face was all teeth. "Where did you get this?" he asked.

"It's my brother's," I said. "I wrote it down, but he figured it out. Except for the freshmen. They're mine. We should be able to run on anybody in the league."

I'd arranged the pitchers by team and he was looking at the kids from Ryder. "Even them," I said.

"This is incredible. How did you—how did he know what to look for?"

"My dad used to play for the Pirates. For their farm teams. He taught us a lot of stuff."

"I didn't know your dad played ball," he said. "I'd like to meet him sometime."

I didn't tell him that my dad was the guy who stood near the first-base fence every day. If he wanted to be a spook, that was okay with me. "You can look through that, but I need it back," I said. "I'm gonna hit."

"Five bunts," he said.

No one has to remind me to drag bunt. It is my favorite part of hitting. When a pitcher seems too tough, I'd just try to nudge one of his fastballs somewhere between first base and the mound. The object is to push it just deep enough so that the pitcher, the first baseman, and the second baseman can't figure out who should field the ball and who should cover the base. By the time they work it out, you're already on. I put down ten bunts, then took my regular cuts.

When Sal let everybody go for the day, Kenny and I stuck around. We always stayed late to practice our double plays, but that day, no one wanted to hit to us, so we

164

spent about half an hour knocking grounders at each other. The first couple weeks of practice I'd felt a little shaky in the field, but when I backhanded one way behind second, I knew I was ready to play.

"That's it for me," Kenny said. "You too. Your ride is here."

A blue Tempo coasted through the parking lot on the left-field line. It was the McDonoughs' car and I figured Annie had stopped by during her driver's lesson. Then she cut the engine and started pounding on the horn. That's when I saw that she was alone.

It was nearly twilight when Annie hopped the fence and jogged across the infield. I could see this look of surprise and satisfaction on her face.

"I did it," she yelled. "I did it." Kenny gave her a high-five, like she'd just hit a home run.

Sometimes when something terrific happens to you, you don't really realize at the time, and later you wish that you'd remembered it better. But other times you know you're doing something great, so you pull back a little and watch yourself doing it. In my mind I was watching myself hugging Annie when I suddenly saw us captured in a car commercial.

You know the kind I mean. Gentle music, happy people, soft lighting, and this gorgeous sky. It looks like a special moment in a real life, except that it's not real life and you hate them for pretending it is. Because how can you ever learn to feel your own feelings if the people on television keep stealing them from you? You want to believe that your moment is unique and that no one will ever know exactly how you feel, but somebody already does

165

know, and they're using the knowledge to sell Chevrolets. It's the heartbeat of America.

I stopped watching myself hug Annie and just concentrated on the hug.

"It was so easy this time," she said. "I can't believe how easy it was. Who needs a ride?"

"The Dunham-mobile is on the prowl," Kenny said, and we ran for the car.

Annie drove like she had a trunk full of heirlooms. "You guys are my first passengers," she said.

After we dropped Kenny at his house this mischievous look came into her eyes. "Let's go for a ride."

"As long as you promise not to take advantage of me," I said.

She followed Boulevard Avenue to Route 81 and pointed us south toward Darden. Every time the transmission kicked up a gear she looked at me surprised, like she wasn't the one who was doing it.

"Fifty miles an hour," she said. "We're going fifty miles an hour." After about five minutes on the highway she decided she was going to pass someone.

"Blinker on," I narrated. "No one in the mirror. A quick glance over the shoulder and . . ."

"Cut it out," she said, laughing. "I'm trying to *drive.*"

In the passing lane she zipped by an older guy in a Pacer and some lady with a station wagon full of kids. "Fifty-eight miles an hour," she said. "I'm speeding."

For some reason that got me thinking about the accident. It felt like we were riding along inside it, but that it wasn't really touching us. I pictured it like this huge bubble you could live inside, but never see. And I wondered

166

if we would always live inside it, or if one day we'd try to make it pop. Halfway to Darden she turned the car around and headed home.

"I'm not sure how this works," I said when she pulled up in front of my house. "Can I ask you for a date in *your* car, or do you have to ask me?"

"You have to wait," she said.

"How long?"

She looked out the window and hummed about fifteen seconds worth of "As Time Goes By." And then she asked, "Busy Friday night?"

"Nothing I can't cancel."

"Pick you up at seven thirty," she said.

"You're on a roll, Connely," I told myself climbing the stairs to the house. "A definite roll."

I have warned myself against getting carried away like that, but it never seems to work. Right after another silent dinner with Dad, Charley called and I realized that nothing was over yet.

"Gotta talk to you, man," he said.

"What's up?"

"Everything," he said. "Everything is up for grabs."

I'd only seen him once in the three weeks since he saved my ass in front of Lucy's, but still it was unusual for him to call me. I told Mom I had to bring a book over to somebody from school. "It might take a while," I said. "He was sick for the whole lesson."

The Cowboy showed up on his motorcycle.

"Where's the Biscayne?" I asked.

"You'll see," he said.

Charley dropped low on every curve between my house

and his. I held tight and tried not to think of the asphalt inches below my kneecaps. We were there in no time.

From the road I could see that his house had been smeared with black paint. Somebody had painted *Ghostbuster*-type symbols all over it. That wasn't all. Both windshields of the Biscayne were smashed to pieces. The little shed where he used to keep the cycle was kicked in like a cardboard box. The roof sat on the rubble about two feet off the ground.

"Home sweet fuckin' home," he said, getting off the cycle at the top of the drive.

"What happened?"

"Looks like I had a few visitors last night when I was out."

"You tell the cops?"

"It coulda *been* the cops."

He unlocked the door. The inside of his house was okay, but all the records had been packed into crates.

"Is this all 'cause of me?" I said. " 'Cause of Mark Ryder?"

"I don't know. Could be. Could be because I've been spending a little time with Richie Munley."

"What for?"

He was at the refrigerator popping open a Molson. "No thanks," I said, and took a seat at the table.

"When I was at Bucknell, sophomore year," he said, "I had a couple of philosophy classes with this guy John Collins who was a big wheel at the school paper. A couple of months ago I started seeing his stuff in the *Inquirer.* "

I saw what was coming.

"I gave him a call and told him what was up. He just

started down there, so he's covering the hinterlands. This could be a pretty big story for him."

"What did you tell him?"

"I told him what you told me. He says he needs two people, Richie Munley and your dad."

"Why my dad?"

"He figures that whoever spilled it to your dad might be willing to spill it to him. Maybe somebody has an axe to grind with Uncle Sheriff."

"How are you going to get to Richie?"

"I'll tell you, old Richie is as fucked up about this as anybody. His one friend is dead. The other one ain't talking to him. He can't play ball and he never knows when that money is coming. He wouldn't mind crawling out of this. I just have to keep my eye on him."

"My dad won't talk about it," I said.

"Talk to him."

"I can't, Charley. It's like the guy is falling apart. He hardly even speaks to me anymore."

"BC, we might only get the one shot at this."

"He's not going to say anything," I said. "It would be a horror show for him. He'd lose his job. People would find out he was juicing and everybody would think he was an asshole for letting it happen in the first place."

"Gotta try, man."

"Why? What are you doing this for?" I said.

"My outraged sense of justice."

"It's not funny."

He was sitting at the table with his feet propped up on the sink. After a long drag on his Molson, he looked at his boots. "I'm moving out of here," he said.

"What? Where?"

"School. Going back to school."

"You said school was bullshit."

"It is bullshit," he said, standing up. "Most of it. Thing is, they don't let you do anything if you don't do school first. I didn't mind that for a while because there was nothing I wanted to do. This was a pretty good time, here, but it gets old."

"You're afraid," I said.

That didn't bother him as much as I hoped it would. "I'm just tired, BC. I've made all the tapes I can make. I'm runnin' out of places to hang out. It's time to go."

He walked over to the front windows. For a second I thought maybe there was somebody outside. I think he thought so, too.

"This is ridiculous," he said. "One night I get home and some high school kids have painted my house for me, smashed my windshields, and all I can do is maybe go and kick their asses around. Daddy runs this. Uncle runs that. Shit, I'm gonna be twenty-four, BC. That's too old to be beating up high school kids in parking lots."

When you look up to people, I guess you block out the stuff that might be wrong with them. Then, either gradually, like with my dad, or all at once, like with Charley, you find out what that stuff is. That should probably help you understand them better, but actually it just makes you scared. It feels like somebody has just pulled out one of your tent poles, and all you can think of is that the tent is going to cave in on you.

"Don't leave yet," I said.

"It sucks around here," Charley said. He came over and

170

stood near my chair. "Sooner or later the Ryders are gonna get you and you won't be able to breathe unless you're on their side."

He shoved both hands in his pockets and stood there shaking his head. "But I just want this one last shot at them. You know what I mean?"

I knew what he meant. I knew what he meant all the way back to the night in the parking lot when he told me that it wasn't just about me and my parents anymore. But it still didn't seem fair. First we were victims of a lie and now we were going to be victims of the truth.

"I'll talk to my dad," I said, but I didn't know whether I meant it or not.

20

Sal was an ogre again the next day at practice. We did extra calisthenics. We ran extra wind sprints. Every time anybody did anything wrong he screamed at them.

"I wonder what this is about?" Kenny said when we were waiting to hit.

"I think he feels the season closing in," I said.

"I think his wife is starching his jockeys." Kenny did this little stiff-legged walk we called The Martinelli and we both shot a guilty glance at Sal.

"How 'bout you?" Kenny asked.

"My jockeys fit fine," I said.

"Not too tight?"

I looked at him pretty hard. "No," I said, because I didn't feel like telling the truth.

"Mine are cutting off my circulation," he said.

Kenny had a knack for putting me on, but I could see

on his face that this time he wasn't fooling. Half the school had been talking about the "new black star." He was the only reason most kids cared about the team. Pretty soon it would be time to produce. I never knew it bothered him. Before I could say anything he Martinellied up to the plate to take his cuts.

After three hours, Sal called us into a huddle along the first-base line. "I know I was a little hard on you guys today," he said. "And I'm sorry." He pulled a few sheets of paper from his back pocket and waved them at us. "We got our schedule yesterday."

A couple of the guys cheered. "Let's get 'em," Eddie Ciccone said.

"You guys know I have a lot of confidence in you," Sal said. "We're a young team. We're only going to get better the longer we're together. I want you to remember that all season long."

Come on, Sal, I was thinking, out with it.

"I'll be honest with you guys. I was hoping for a better break from the schedule. We open the season next Wednesday—against Ryder. . . ."

I felt like someone had just told me my plane was going to crash. All the awful possibilities flashed through my mind. Mark Ryder striking me out. Mark Ryder hitting a home run. The Wildcats kicking our asses in front of everybody I ever knew. Last year when *I* was a Wildcat, we'd beaten Reese Point 17–2 and Sherrill played the freshmen for three innings. Maybe it was time to catch a cold.

"As of right now we start preparing for that game," Sal said. "I don't have to tell you that they are tough. They're a bigger school. They have a stronger tradition. But I'd like to think we're starting a tradition right here with you guys. I expect a good showing and if they look past us . . ."

We're usually a pretty jovial bunch, but that day practice broke up real quietly. Even Ciccone couldn't muster up any false macho bullshit.

I don't know why it hit me so hard. I knew we were going to have to play them sooner or later. But not this sooner. At home I called Annie to tell her about it and she got frantic that Mark Ryder would throw at my head.

"That's the same day that reporter is coming," I said.

"Did you talk to your dad about it yet?"

"No. Guess I better, huh?"

"Bobby, They don't know about—us, do they?"

"Not yet. They don't know about you and they don't know that I told Mark Ryder and they *definitely* don't know anything about this reporter coming."

"What do you think will happen?"

"Don't worry," I said. Half the time, when you tell someone not to worry, you are a mess yourself.

I was going to spill the beans at dinner, but I didn't know how to bring it up. "Dad, how would you like to expose all your gravest failures to a huge newspaper audience?" didn't seem like quite the ticket. Maybe something casual would be better, like, "I heard a reporter was coming to town to talk to Richie Munley about the accident." But that would make them paranoid. Besides, it wasn't enough. It left out Mark Ryder. And it left out Annie.

Most nights after dinner Mom does the dishes while Dad has another cup of coffee. Then either Dad dries or else I do. But that night, as soon as the plates were in the sink, Dad tromped upstairs and came back down with two manila envelopes filled with bills.

For some reason I thought I might still be able to get a word in, so I fixed myself a cup of tea and sat at the other end of the table. The bills were always a pain in the ass, but I'd never seen Dad sweat them the way he did that night. He'd copy down a bunch of figures from one envelope, punch them into the calculator, copy down a bunch of figures from the other envelope, punch those into the calculator, and then go back and do it all over again. I think I was making him nervous just by sitting there.

He was in the middle of the world's longest grimace when I climbed the stairs to do my homework. That wasn't much help. You can only think about osmosis and cotangents for so long when you're going crazy. After about two hours not even *Animal Farm* was holding my attention. For some reason I felt like I needed an excuse to go downstairs, so I decided I was hungry.

Dad was still hacking away at the calculator when I opened the refrigerator to grab an orange. Mom was in the living room watching *Cagney and Lacey.* She loves Mary Beth, the cop with the three kids.

"She might have cancer," she said when I peeked in.

"Who might?"

"Mary Bett." She said it with a New York accent, like Mary Beth's husband.

"Want some?" I said, holding out the orange.

"Shhh."

I waited for a commercial before I asked her what was going on in the kitchen.

"Your father has a lot on his mind," she said.

"I sort of do, too."

She waited for me to say something, but I couldn't get started. "Honey, what is it. Is something wrong?"

"No, I just . . ."

"Tell me."

"I need to tell you both."

"Come on. The bills can wait."

"Bill," she said and led me into the kitchen. "Bobby has something he wants to talk to us about." She pulled out a chair and sat down beside him. My father glanced up at me, and put down his pencil. "What's up?" he said.

This felt the way it did right after Billy died, when we talked like this about once a week. It was the shrink's idea. My parents had exactly the same kind of nervous looks on their faces.

I sat down with my arms across the back of a chair and started to talk without really knowing where I was going: "I have these two friends that you guys don't know about. Well, you sort of know about the one, Charley, but you definitely don't know about the other one. After I found out what happened to Billy, I was freaking out and I needed to tell somebody, so I ended up telling it to them."

They had to have been expecting that much because it didn't seem to bother them. Or maybe they already knew about this, too.

I told them about coming home that night, without mentioning that I'd been to Darden, and I told about seeing Mark Ryder and telling him that I knew. My father was nodding.

"I guess you probably heard about that," I said. "After

176

I told him he jumped me, and Charley came ripping out of this bar across the street to help me out. He wanted to know why we were fighting, so I figured I should tell him."

Dad was shaking his head and gritting his teeth. Mom had a blank expression on her face. They were already pissed off and I hadn't even said a word about the reporter.

When I told them what Charley had done, my father pushed his chair back from the table and hung his head. I was afraid he was going to start screaming. My mom's eyes filled up.

"He wants to come here and talk to us, mostly to Dad," I said. "He thinks that if you tell him about what the cops in Tamble Ridge told you, then maybe he can get them to tell him, too. I know everything would have to come out then, but I thought . . ." But I didn't know what I thought, so I just shut up and stared at Dad's calculator. I almost wanted him to yell but he didn't say anything. He didn't even look at me.

"I guess that's it," I said after a while. "Good night."

From the bottom of the stairs I heard my mother call, "Bobby. Who's your other friend?"

"Annie Dunham," I said.

She didn't exactly bolt up the stairs after me, but as soon as I was in bed, she knocked on the door and shuffled across the room.

"We're trying to do the right thing," she said, sitting on the edge of the bed and folding her hands in her lap. "You know what this would be like for your father if it ever came out?"

"I told them he probably wouldn't do it," I said.

"You shouldn't give up on him so easily."

"Do you think he *will*?"

"I don't know," she said. "I just don't want you to—to think that he can't do the right thing."

"Do *you* think it would be the right thing?"

Mom leaned back on the bed and began rubbing my feet through the blankets. I couldn't tell if she hadn't made up her mind yet, or if she just didn't want to hurt anybody. For a long time she looked thoughtful, then she smiled like she'd just remembered a joke.

"So," she said, "this Annie Dunham, is she a nice girl?"

Diving

He was just about packed when I came home from the wedding I'd served that morning. My dad's old Army footlocker was open on the bed, all filled up with sweat socks and sweat pants and T-shirts and jerseys.

"How'd you do?" he asked.

"Five bucks," I said.

I hung my cassock and surplice in the closet and stretched out on my bed. This was a pretty familiar feeling. Here goes Billy again. Billy the pioneer. This was going to happen for the rest of our lives. Billy would go to college. He'd get a job. He'd move away. He'd get married. He'd have kids. And just as soon as I caught up, he'd go on to the next thing, whatever that was.

He was a nervous wreck, though. Maybe he thought his chances of getting out of town depended on that one week. Maybe he was right.

"Gotta kick ass this week," he said, facing the foot-locker.

"You will."

"If Blackie remembers who I am by the end of camp, then I'll be all set. Somebody will definitely have a ride for me."

Ride meant scholarship. "It would be great to play for Blackie," I said. "Then we could come down and see you."

"I gotta kick ass."

"You'll do great."

I didn't think there was any question about it, but he just shrugged his shoulders and kept balling socks. For some reason he wouldn't turn around, so after a while, I left the room.

21

The day of the Ryder game was as crisp and clear as anything early April is allowed to give you. The sun was so bright we wore lampblack beneath our eyes. The air was so warm that the bat didn't sting in your hands if you made lousy contact. Nice day for a massacre, I thought.

I'd hardly slept the night before. I didn't figure we could beat Ryder, but maybe at least we'd make it close. As long as we didn't embarrass ourselves. There'd be a lot of people at the game who were pretty cold to us after the accident. There were a lot of guys on that team who forgot how much my brother used to mean to them. And there were a lot of people who laughed at us just because we were Reese Point and we hadn't beaten Ryder at anything since people listened to the Bee Gees.

Thinking about the game made me nervous, but so did thinking about everything else. The Cowboy's friend came to town that night. He was seeing Richie Munley the next afternoon and he wanted to come to our house right after the game. On top of that, my mother kept saying how much she was looking forward to meeting Annie. I wasn't looking forward to that at all.

When I was a kid, I tried to convince God to send me secret messages disguised as baseball scores. "If the Mets win this game I'll get an A in geography." "If the Yankees win this game I won't have to serve any Masses with Monsignor Bryant." By the time the two-A.M. whistle blew at the Ash I was trying to talk him into the same kind of deal. "If we don't get blown out, Dad will talk to the reporter." "If we don't get blown out, Charley will stick around."

It was depressing to know that there was nothing I could do about the really important stuff that was going to happen the next day, but after a while that made me grateful for the one thing I could do: play ball.

My parents were as tense as I was. When Mom rattled some pots in the kitchen the next morning, Dad and I jumped back from the table like the I-beam had snapped. All day in class I kept making notes about where their guys liked to hit the ball. Sal came into fifth-period lunch and sat in the corner with Ratch talking about how to pitch their hitters. By social studies I was *Night of the Living Dead* material.

"Hey, Connely," Annie said in the hallway. "Wait up."

"Hi. Sorry. I'm all zoned out."

"Don't worry, you'll be great."

"You know," I said, "what if that newspaper guy wants to talk to you and your aunt and uncle?"

182

"Will you calm down? You can't take care of every single problem, you know."

"What if we stink?" I said. "What if *I* stink?"

"I'll probably quit hanging around with you," she said. "Come on, lighten up. I got something for you." Digging into her purse, she came out with a tiny green shamrock that had a red heart stitched in the middle. Some local politician had used them last November instead of campaign buttons. I think he lost. "It's good luck," she said.

"We'll need it."

"Connely, *relax.*"

But I didn't, and nobody else did either. In the locker room we all dressed real slowly. Hardly anybody said a word. Eddie Ciccone lumbered in yelling, "Here we go, Blue Jays. Here we go," but nobody paid any attention to him. I'd served livelier funerals.

Kenny was the last guy to show up. He pushed through the door doing his Groucho Marx walk and stopped in the middle of the room. Looking around at everybody, he cupped a hand to his ear and started talking like Scotty on *Star Trek*. "Captain, I don't hear any noise down there, Captain. Are ya all right?"

We all just sort of looked at him funny, so he bounced over to his locker and started shrieking.

"The *new* unis. They are just *too* divine. Look at these sleeves. Would you say royal? I'd say royal. Or perhaps it's sapphire. Ex*act*ly. Sapphire. And that gray flannel, always in style."

He charged over to Danny Ratchford, who was wearing his jock and a sweatshirt.

"Here we see Danny in a lovely little smock. Slims the

183

hips, accentuates the bust, and certainly makes no secret of the star pitcher's *manly* biceps."

Pat Carr was standing a couple of feet away. He had pulled his jersey on over his sweatshirt. "Now Pat here is re*splen*dent in the smock-and-jumper combo," Kenny said. "The classic gray, so businesslike, but the white numerals, just a tad more playful, if you know what I mean."

Tommy Paultz had stepped into his pants by the time Kenny got to him. "Will you look at this," he sang. "The sleek lines. The dashing sapphire piping. *Here* is a man of action."

That's when 185 pounds worth of Johnny Dukus came prancing across the room, wearing nothing but his cup and stirrup socks. Duker hit him with a modeling pose.

"And of course Dukus, the mysterious model who goes by a single name, is ever so elegant, ever so sophisticated. Can we have a camera over here, please."

Kenny draped an arm over Johnny's shoulder, pulled a pen out of his pocket, and started talking into it like it was a microphone.

"Ah, Dukus, in these accessories would you say you're ready for action?"

"I'm ready for anything," Duker said, rolling his hips.

"Are you ready to kick some ass?"

"Yeah."

"I think the folks at home would like to hear you say so."

"I'm ready to kick some ass," Johnny shouted.

"And you, Mr. Ciccone?"

"I'm ready to kick some ass," Eddie yelled.

"How about you, Bobby?"

"I'm ready to kick some ass," I said.

He asked about five more guys and everybody said the same thing. Kenny quit talking like a fashion critic and roared at us like a preacher. "All together now. Let me hear you. What are we gonna do?"

"Kick some ass," everybody shouted.

Just that second Mr. Kelsey walked in. It was hard to tell who was more more embarrassed, him or us.

"Well boys, men," he said, looking at the floor, which is where everyone else was looking too, "I just came down to wish you good luck."

"Thank you, Mr. Kelsey," we all said at once.

He hurried out the door with Tommy Paultz right behind him. Tommy peeked up the hallway and raised his hand like he was going to start a race. When Kelsey rounded the corner, Tommy dropped the flag and everybody broke up.

22

We were feeling sort of optimistic as the game began. First, we found out that Coach Sherrill had decided not to waste Mark Ryder, his best pitcher, against us. Then Ratch faced their four best hitters and held them scoreless in the first. I was all for calling it a moral victory and getting the hell out of there. But things kept getting better.

Kenny cracked a single into left field leading off our first. "Let's get to work, Bobby," Sal yelled. I dropped the other bat I was swinging and walked to the plate.

All week long Kenny and I had worked on a personal set of signals. If I held the bat down on the knob it meant I was taking the pitch. If I choked up, but slid my bottom hand up and down, that meant I was bunting. If I didn't do either of those things, I was swinging away.

I started out down on the knob, giving Kenny a chance to steal a base on Ronnie Yannis, the Ryder pitcher.

Ronnie tips his head backward a little just before his pick-off move. Kenny had read Billy's book so he knew that. On the first pitch he got a jump so big that he went into second base standing.

I stepped out and looked at Sal in the dugout. He flashed me the bunt sign. I figured it was a decent enough move. Even if they got me out, we'd have Kenny at third and the heart of our order due up.

That's about how it worked out. Yannis scooped up my bunt and tagged me as I ran past, but Kenny hustled into third. When Pat Carr hit a sky-high sacrifice fly, we led 1–0.

Our dugout went nuts. I was standing next to Ratch, who started braying like a mad donkey. "We. Lead. Ryder," Tommy Paultz kept shouting. "We. Lead. Ryder."

The fans gave us this huge ovation when the inning was over. The bleachers were nearly filled, maybe three hundred people. Half of them were probably from Ryder, but for the time being, that was okay with me.

Ratch put them down in order in the second. My first chance was an easy one-hopper, the kind I'd been fielding since Little League.

Between pitches I checked out the crowd. Annie was right behind our dugout sitting with Kenny's sister Bev and some kids from the history club. Our eyes met for a second and she waved her hands over her head.

I couldn't find my parents until the top of the third. A foul ball up the first-base line crashed into the crowd near my mother. It struck me kind of funny that she was there by herself, because Dad almost never missed a game. I tried not to worry about that, but it didn't do much good.

We were still ahead when I came up with one out in the third and smacked Yannis's first pitch into left field for a single. Rounding first, I took a wide turn and tried to draw a throw, but it didn't work. Mark Ryder slapped me with a tag anyway.

I'd made up my mind not to say anything, but I shot him a quick look just to let him know I thought he was an asshole. "Whatsa matter, can't you take it?" he said. I didn't answer, but he got on me about that, too. "You keep quiet like a good little boy," he said.

While he bothered me, I bothered Yannis. Ronnie tried to pick me off twice, but both times I got back standing up. Ryder kept whacking me with the tag. I was hoping I could steal this damn base before my whole body was black and blue.

"I guess you'll be real quiet now that we took care of your friend," he said. I looked at him just long enough to see his smile. It made me wonder if he was bragging about the paint job, or if something else had happened.

I took a longer lead. Yannis kept looking at me, so I faked a dash toward second. He stepped off the rubber. "Got him now," I thought.

Finally, Ronnie decided to stop worrying about me. As soon as he pitched, I took off.

A split second later I heard the crack of the bat and knew that Pat Carr had really belted one. The ball whizzed behind me just as I sped for second. I heard the crowd "Oooooh," but suddenly the sound died in their throats.

Behind me, Mark Ryder had made a diving catch.

When I turned he was flat on his stomach near the right-field line, clutching the ball in his glove. He beat me back to the bag easily to finish off the double play.

"Nice running, Speedboat," he said, when I jogged past.

Imagine you're a tightrope walker and right in the middle of your act somebody reminds you that you're afraid of heights. That's about the effect that the double play had on us. Eddie Ciccone booted Ryder's grounder to open the fourth. Ratch got a little testy and walked Pete Nellis. One out later they had runners on second and third. I figured it was as good a time to fall apart as any.

Ronnie Yannis blasted the first pitch Ratch threw. The ball shot off his bat so fast that Kenny barely had time to move. Everything that happened next seemed like a highlight film to me.

Kenny took a step to his left and lunged. For a split second he hung in the air, reaching with his glove hand, like some flying waiter balancing a tray.

The ball was slicing away from him, but when it hit the top of his webbing, it kicked straight up into the air. Both he and the ball began dropping at once. I know this is weird, but I thought of that experiment by Galileo. The thing was, this time, it didn't work out. The ball fell faster. It's like Kenny was a fugitive from the law of gravity. Just before he hit the ground, he took another swipe at it. The ball disappeared inside his glove.

I was so enthralled that I almost forgot to cover second. It seemed like we should observe a moment of silence or something. Luckily enough, Pete Nellis was halfway to third base, so we had no trouble doubling him off.

If we had scored that inning we could have put that

game away. Everybody felt it when we came tearing in off the field. "Their ass is grass and we're lawnmowers," Eddie Ciccone said. "Let's do a little damage," Sal shouted. Our guys went up there like lions in the fourth inning.

They made outs like lambs.

Poor Ratch was pitching his ass off and all we'd gotten him was one lousy run. I didn't think he could keep it up much longer, but he set them down in the fifth.

I got to wishing that Dad would show up while we were still leading, so he could appreciate the scrap we were giving them. I thought Kenny's play would have put him in mind of Billy, the way that watching that Gillespie kid had. That was kind of a nice idea at first, but after a while it bothered me. How come he could get such a kick out of a stranger when he wouldn't even come to see me play?

Running off the field that inning, I heard somebody at the fence yell my name. The voice came from this young guy in gray pants, a button-down shirt, and a yellow tie. He wanted to know if I was who I was, so I said yeah. He was John Collins, which I figured out before he told me. Nobody from around here wears yellow ties.

"Where's Charley?" I asked.

Collins shook his head. "He's in jail," he said.

It felt like somebody had just taken a bat to the back of my neck. I was still looking at this guy, but I swear I was completely out of it. My father was missing. Charley was in jail. What the hell was going on?

"He was supposed to bring that Munley kid to meet me

190

at a diner," Collins said. "I guess the sheriff caught up with them first. They're holding him on possession of narcotics and possession of a firearm."

"Charley doesn't have a gun," I said.

"He probably didn't have any pot on him either unless it was planted," Collins said. "Munley was released right away. Into the custody of his father, so that angle is shot. I think they'd like to keep Charley overnight, but we've got an attorney from my paper on the phone with them now. I'm not sure they can get away with it."

He stopped for a second and looked around the park. "Course it seems as though they get away with whatever they want."

That stung the way it always stings when a stranger tells you the truth about yourself. You know he's right, but it still pisses you off that he said so.

"How did they know?"

"I don't know," he said. "It could be that Munley broke down. Or it could be that somebody who knew I was coming tipped them off." He looked at me hard, but I didn't catch on right away.

All of a sudden I felt weightless. It felt like half the people I cared about were drifting out in space somewhere and I couldn't touch them. There was Charley who got nabbed, right before he was going to make his getaway. And there was Dad, who got cut off, before he even had his chance to tell the truth, and out there somewhere was Billy, waiting for people to know what really happened. Only nobody ever would.

"I guess that's the end of it then," I said. I wanted to

cry, but I didn't like this guy and I wasn't going to let him see me do that.

"Unless I can talk to your dad." He made it sound like that was a hilarious idea.

"He's not here yet," I said.

Collins raised an eyebrow and took a seat. I sat on the bench and started wondering what would happen to Charley. Mom and Dad and I were the only other people who knew he was coming to town. He couldn't think that *I* tipped off the sheriff. Then I thought of how he laughed when he said, "Unless I can talk to your dad."

I looked up in the stands after just about every pitch the next inning. Mom was still sitting by herself. "It couldn't have been him," I kept saying to myself. But after a while, just having to deny it made me wonder.

23

I kept smoothing the infield dirt with my spikes and telling myself to keep my mind on the game. But things weren't looking too bright on the field either. With one out in the sixth, and Mark Ryder up, Ratch decided he was about to throw the world's hottest fastball.

Ryder crushed it.

The ball took off on this huge arc into right field. Chris Welch didn't even try to keep his eye on it. He just turned around and tore ass after it. There is no fence around our field, but the land breaks downhill out in right about 375 feet from the plate. The ball hit just shy of the slope and bounced down. I ran out to take the cutoff throw, but Ryder could have been around another time or two before we got it back to the infield.

Their half of the fans were better at making noise than ours. They went wild for what seemed like an hour. I started to feel like we were playing in a foreign country. "We may not get out of this alive," I thought.

But somehow we did. They hit bullets that inning, but they hit them right at us and it was still 1–1 when we came up to bat.

"This is our chance to win this one," Sal shouted as we came off the field. Let's go, eight, nine, one."

The truth was that Kenny was our only decent hitter due up that inning. If he got on base maybe I'd have a chance to hit him in. After Welchy struck out I grabbed a bat and stepped out of the dugout. Up the right-field line I found my mother. Sitting beside her was John Collins.

I wanted to kill that bastard. He was doing most of the talking. She just sat there shaking her head, like she didn't want to be seen with him. I thought about running up there and dragging him out of the stands by his yellow tie. *God damn it.* This was Charley's fault. But Charley was in jail and that must be somebody's fault, too. Maybe somehow it was even mine.

Kenny bounced a two-out single past shortstop and I heard people call my name. "Let's go, Connely," Annie screamed. I made the mistake of looking at her.

You can fight your feelings for a long time when there is nobody to tell them to. But once you have somebody, you want them all the time, especially when you are in trouble. I headed up to the plate wishing I was heading into the stands. I was also wishing that my dad would show up, because that way at least I'd know.

Strike one was just above the knees on the outside corner.

194

I stepped out and glanced up the right-field line. Among all the shifting figures I found my father. He was picking his way toward Mom's seat.

Ball one was waist high, but inside.

I saw John Collins stand up to shake Dad's hand, but then I lost them in a mass of faces that were all looking straight at me.

Strike two was letter high. Kenny stole second, but I didn't notice until I looked out and saw him standing there. On the right-field line my father sat down. John Collins was nowhere in sight. It should be possible to call time-out when you think your life is being ruined.

Strike three was right down the middle, but I didn't even cock my bat. I think I might have kept walking right past the dugout and out into the stands except that Kenny caught up with me at the door.

"What's the matter?" he said.

"Nothing, I just choked, that's all."

"You didn't give me a signal or nothin'."

"Leave me alone, all right?"

"What's the matter?"

"Butt out."

Luckily for me, nothing came my way in the seventh, because I was out there in a daze. If the Cowboy was in jail because of Dad, I was never going home again. In my mind I had this little picture of myself sitting in the window of a dorm at DSU. Maybe that wasn't what would happen, but I wouldn't end up around here. No matter what, I wouldn't end up around here.

It was the cheering that snapped me out of it. Eddie

195

Ciccone had just settled under a pop-up outside third. Their half of the inning was over. "This is it," Sal yelled. "Three, four, five. Let's go home happy."

The guys were in a frenzy. They celebrated every pitch outside the strike zone. For a minute it looked like we might actually pull it out. Not that I cared. I just kept looking up the right-field line for my father and wondering where he'd been. It seemed like my whole life depended on it.

With one out, Dukus doubled. Tommy Paultz walked, but Ratch popped up. That brought up Eddie Ciccone with the winning run on second.

Half the town had shown up by that point and everybody was screaming for him. He must love this, I thought. I almost wished he'd make an out, and when he did, I felt guilty. Eddie just froze up there. It was a 2-and-2 fastball that caught him looking. "At least we have something in common," I thought.

I was way wrong about that, though. Old hot-shit Eddie came back to the dugout with tears in his eyes. His bat clattered on the floor. "I'm sorry," he said to Sal. "I'm sorry, everybody. I thought it was outside."

A couple of guys patted him on the ass, but I just sat there looking at him. Eddie was the bane of my existence. He was on everybody's All-Asshole team. First string. But here he was playing his rocks off while I sat around licking my wounds. There's some shit you'll let yourself get away with and there's some that you won't. Having Eddie Ciccone try harder than you is definitely in the second category.

"It's okay, Eddie," I said. "We'll get 'em."

"Can you go one more inning, Ratch?" Sal asked.

"One more."

I was trying hard to get myself pumped up. During warm-ups I kept looking for Annie in the stands. She wasn't with Bev and she wasn't with the kids from the history club. "Great time to go home," I thought.

Without really wanting to, I looked up at where my parents were sitting. I knew I'd try to read some kind of answer in their faces and that would just get me worrying again. But when I found them, the stuff about Charley never entered my mind. Sitting to Mom's left was Annie. She saw me looking her way and gave me a one-person standing ovation.

I didn't want to think about how right that looked. Somebody who didn't know any better might check us out and figure he was dealing with a Norman Rockwell painting. I mean, here was this kid on a baseball field in the late afternoon sun, and there was his girlfriend standing up to cheer for him. Both his parents were there. Hell, everybody's parents were there. It looked like the whole damn community was in love with this game.

Yeah, we'd fool the pants right off him. *"Carve up that apple pie, Grandma,"* he'd say. *"This here is a great country we live in."*

Of course the picture wouldn't have the dead brother in it, or the buried secrets. And you couldn't tell that all the boy and girl ever talked about was getting out of town. There wouldn't be any way of knowing who was taking the bribes and who was paying them off. You couldn't tell

197

how long that had been going on, or whether it was something in the water that made everybody else dopey enough to let it continue.

I'm not saying that what happened next was on a par with God knocking Saint Paul off his horse or anything, but standing behind second base, waiting for Duker's practice throw, I realized that I knew what I knew. Maybe the whole town would never find it out, but that was their own fault. I knew it and I'd never act like I didn't. And Annie knew it too. We were looking at the same picture as everybody else, but it seemed different to us. I pounded my glove and felt the shamrock where I'd pasted it inside.

Ratch walked Roger Murphy leading off the eighth.

For the rest of the inning I felt like I had two different brains going. The one was watching every little detail on every pitch, but the other was racing along on a road I'd never seen before. I guess you don't have too much control over what you see when that happens. But I didn't mind so much because all I kept seeing was Annie. *Annie out on the steeple at Holy Angels. Annie crying at the park. Annie with the popcorn in the movies.*

Ratch threw over twice to keep Murphy close.

Annie on the chair with the crooked golden slipcover. Annie with the Jackie Robinson book.

As soon as Ratch went to the plate Roger lit out for second and I lit out to cover. Duker's throw skipped up to me on a short hop, but I squeezed it hard. Roger's spikes sprayed dirt. I slapped him on the ankle, but he was safe.

Annie with the steam rising around her face. Annie with

the now-or-never look in her eyes. Annie asleep on my shoulder on the Levinskis' couch.

Scott Phillips hit second for Ryder. He choked way up on the bat and laid down a beautiful bunt. Tommy charged and I hurried over to cover first. Ratch knocked the ball down, but lost his balance and fell. Flat on his ass, he snapped off a throw that beat Phillips by half a step. Murphy pulled into third. Mark Ryder was up.

"Fifty-eight miles an hour. I'm speeding." Annie on my lap in the front seat, because the backseat was for bad girls. Annie with the shamrock. It's scary when your memory behaves like a music video.

The crowd was buzzing like a field full of cicadas. Sal motioned for Ratch to give Ryder an intentional walk. Ratch threw four intentional balls to Ryder while their fans booed.

I took a quick look at the stands. Dad was on his feet. Annie and my mother were holding hands. I still didn't know what my father had done, or how my mother felt about it, but at least I was one for three up there.

Duker flashed signs. Kenny moved one step to his right. Pete Nellis took the first pitch for a ball.

"It sort of seems like you might be in love with Annie Dunham," I said to myself. As usual, my timing sucked.

Ratch threw over to first, but Ryder got back. Nellis swung through the 1-and-0 pitch.

"But how can you know if you're in love with somebody when you've never been in love before?"

Nellis fouled one back, 1 and 1.

I guess you just know, I thought. Or maybe I was about

to think that when Duker set up inside and I took a step to my right.

Pete Nellis swung hard and clubbed this angry snake of a ground ball between short and third. Kenny bolted to his right, gloved the ball, leaped into the air, and snapped off a throw that moved toward me like a balloon against the breeze. While I waited for the ball I could see his mouth moving, but it was too noisy to hear.

Even before I caught the ball, I was ready to jump. Ryder must have been counting on that, because as soon as I stepped on second and turned toward first, there he was—standing straight up and charging right at me. If I threw the ball overhand, I would have broken his nose. I could have splattered his fucking nose all over his fucking face. I'm glad there wasn't any time to think about that.

Everything else was instinct, or maybe it was seven years' worth of playing beside my brother. Anyway, I took a quick half step out of his way and cut loose a throw.

I didn't see what happened after that. Ryder caught me beneath the chin with a football block that knocked me flat on my back. My head hit the ground so hard it bounced and his body rolled over mine.

I must have been out for a second or two, but I must have kept moving, because the next thing I remember is crouching behind the bag on my hands and knees. All our guys were charging toward me. I heard Ryder yelling something and turned to see Kenny driving him to the ground.

Everybody charged onto the field and dove into this huge pile between second and the mound. It looked like somebody had just won the World Series. I saw two guys roll Kenny off Ryder, so I flung myself at them and we all went writhing around in a big ball of arms and legs.

Pretty soon the field was full of coaches and parents just trying to pull us off each other. After Pete Nellis's dad dragged me out of the pile, I found my glove and stood behind second base.

"Hey, Connely," Sal called as he headed toward our bench, "I don't think they want you on their team."

That was the first time I realized that we'd turned the double play.

24

My ears were ringing something ferocious and I felt a fist growing right at the base of my neck. Sal told me I could come out of the game, but I didn't pay any more attention to that than the other guys did to the stuff he said about sportsmanship and the reputation of our school.

Pardon me for saying so, but "Fuck that shit." Ryder cheapshotted me with a thirty-yard head start. If the umpires had any guts they would have thrown him out of the game. But the umpires didn't have any guts, so here he was coming in to pitch the eighth. And there was Kenny, the third guy to face him. It looked like we'd be out there in a big brawling pile again before the inning was over.

I was leaning in the dugout doorway, squeezing a bat and watching the bastard warm up when I heard a voice behind me. "BC."

He's the only one who calls me that, so I knew it was

the Cowboy before I turned around. I would have jumped over the fence and hugged him but I was trying to pay attention while Chris Welch struck out. Besides, he probably would have slugged me.

"This is the gladdest I've ever been to see you," I said.

"We got 'em right where we want 'em, BC," he said. "They are shit scared."

"What are you talking about? We lost Richie, you know."

He just stood there beaming. "Don't need him," he said.

"Why not?"

"We got your dad."

"What?"

"Word down at Uncle Sheriff's office is that he quit his job this afternoon. They weren't too thrilled about it down there."

"Is he—is he gonna talk?"

Charley shrugged. "I wouldn't make any plans for after dinner," he said.

I just about had a stroke. I wanted to laugh or scream or at least prance around a little, but Kevin O'Hora had just whiffed, so it didn't exactly seem like the right time. My dad, I kept thinking, *my* dad.

"You all right?" Ratch asked me.

"Fine, I'm fine."

"So you feel like getting your ass out on deck, or what?"

I spit in my hands, rubbed in a little dirt, and just about moonwalked to the on-deck circle. Looking out to where my dad was sitting, I tried to read relief or conviction or something on his face. But there was nothing there. He looked as uncertain as always.

203

Kenny took Ryder's first pitch for a strike.

I couldn't blame Dad for being uncertain. If the story came out it would hurt him worse than it would hurt the Ryders. The whole secret had always depended on his being more ashamed of it than they were. That and the money.

Ryder tried to get macho with Kenny. He came in tight with a fastball, but missed. It was 1 and 1.

The money was the confusing part. It took me a long time to figure out that it wasn't just about greed. In sort of a twisted way, it was about loyalty, or family, or something—I don't know—*cleaner.* Something you wouldn't mind drawing on your personal coat of arms.

Just to show what a nasty guy he was, Ryder came back inside with another fastball. He missed again. It was 2 and 1.

Dad and Cy Ryder had both done what they'd done for the same reason. Cy Ryder was looking out for his kid and Dad was trying to look out for his. Only Dad had to choose and Cy Ryder didn't. The way my father saw it, he could have the truth for Billy, or a future for me. I guess he figured Billy was already lost, so he let him go again.

Kenny fouled back an off-speed pitch to even the count. The guys on our bench were screaming themselves hoarse. The ringing in my ears got louder and louder.

When I found out about the accident it was sort of like my father lost me, too. It wasn't just the lie that drove me crazy, it was thinking that I was the reason for it and that everything I ever did would be built on it.

Kenny fouled off another pitch, and then another. This

was what TV announcers called a quality at bat. Of course they only called it that if you got on.

I hated my father for what he'd done, and maybe I hated him even more for making me a part of it. But now it seemed like the whole thing was over with. We were going to be free. But as soon as I thought that, I knew it wasn't quite right. We were just going to be free enough to deal with whatever came next.

Ryder was getting frustrated. He kept throwing harder and harder and Kenny kept fouling everything back. His fifth 2-and-2 pitch skipped all the way to the backstop for ball three.

I couldn't imagine how people would react if the story came out. I'd always wanted them to know, but just for Billy's sake, and mine too. Charley wanted them to see it for their own sake, so they'd know what kind of people ran their towns.

Ball four was wide and Kenny took a nice leisurely stroll down to first base.

I think the Cowboy was hoping for a revolution. He wanted people to impeach the sheriff and take over the Ash. I couldn't picture it. Most of them had as much to lose as my father and none of them had as good a reason to lose it. A smaller victory would be just fine with me, although I didn't really know what that victory would look like.

I took my time digging in. I knew that Pat Carr was on deck and that he hadn't hit Mark Ryder in three years of trying. Which meant that somehow, while I was at bat, Kenny had to score from first base.

Ryder was looking in for a sign when I called time-out and pretended there was something in my eye. This was mostly about nerves now and I wanted to do whatever I could to piss him off. His response was a chin-high fastball that sent me spinning down on my hands and knees. I looked up at the umpire. "Let's get the game in," he said.

I could afford to take the next pitch so I slid my grip down to the knob of the bat. Kenny got a big lead.

Ryder threw over, but it wasn't much of a move. People got on base so seldom against him that he never had to learn to keep them close. I took strike one and watched Kenny slide into second ahead of Pete Nellis's throw.

This was about the best situation we could hope for. All I had to do was hit the ball. Yeah, that's *all*.

I dug back in. He took his next sign. I could feel my front knee get wobbly. Strike two was a blur that left me one pitch away from stranding the winning run in scoring position. Again.

It seemed like as good a time to step out as any. This was about par for the course. Another Ryder was about to humiliate another Connely.

"At least I'll get a cut at this one," I told myself and got ready to swing. That's when it hit me.

He had to know I was nervous. He had to know I was ready to swing at just about anything. Why not really make me look bad? Why not throw an off-speed pitch and watch me fall down chasing it? He'd probably tell his *grand*children about that one.

Only I knew.

"Slow curve," I said to myself. "He's gonna throw you a slow curve." I could barely keep from smiling at him.

This was a pitch I could hit. This was a hit I could win the game with. We were going to beat Ryder and I was going to be the hero. I dug back in feeling like Babe Ruth. And that was my mistake.

It was a slow curve, all right, and I laid off until it broke. The damn ball looked bigger than a cantaloupe and my eyes were probably just as wide.

I mashed it. The ball rocketed down the right-field line. Ryder spun to watch it. Kenny streaked toward third. Everybody shot to their feet to see where it would land. I was the only one who knew I'd already blown it. I knew I'd swung too hard and pulled it too much. The ball hit foul by about a foot and a half.

The Reese Point fans all groaned, but the sound may as well have come from me. I'd screwed up on the slow curve and there was no way he was going to throw me another one.

Picking up the bat again, I looked out at the mound. As usual, he was smirking. It made me wonder what it was like to go through life thinking that you always had the trump card. He was getting off on this, especially because it was me. I didn't mind him hating me, I just wished I could use it against him.

In cartoons they always draw light bulbs over people's heads when they have an idea. From what I can tell, it is more like a curtain opening to show what you ought to do. One second I was thinking how I should have busted his face with that throw. The next second, I thought I had a better way to beat him.

Usually when I give Kenny a signal I don't look at him, but this time I did. Staring out to second, I choked the bat and slid my bottom hand up and down the handle: bunt. Just to make sure he saw it, I did it again. He nodded, but I wasn't through. When Sal wants you to keep on running, he moves his head in a circle like he is doing a neck exercise. Before stepping into the box, I did about three or four of those. People must have thought I'd picked a weird time to warm up.

"Getting dark," the umpire said.

I dug back in, stared hard at Ryder, and flashed him this enormous smile. He smiled back. We'll see, I thought.

As the ball streaked in toward the inside half of the plate, I opened my stance, nudged it up the line, and lit out for first.

In certain ways it was the perfect time to bunt. Nobody expects you to lay one down with two strikes on you, because if the ball rolls foul, you're out. I knew the bunt was a good one as soon as I got it down, but I didn't know if it was good enough.

Ronnie Yannis was caught completely by surprise at first. I saw him and Ryder scrambling for it as I ripped up the base line. "Mine," Ryder called. "Mine."

The whole play depended on him fielding the bunt, realizing that I would be safe at first, and holding on to the ball. When I saw their second baseman motioning not to throw, I knew the plan was working.

That's when I went into my banshee act. I rounded first and tore ass for second screaming, "Ryder! Hey Ryder! Ryder! Ryder!"

Most of the field was in front of me now. I saw Kenny take a huge turn at third. Greg Sands, their shortstop, came racing over to cover second. When his eyes got wide,

I knew the ball was on its way and there was nothing else I could do.

By that point I'd stopped running. Thirty feet from second, I slammed on the brakes and yelled "Hey! Hey! Hey! Hey!" just trying to buy a little more time.

Sands knew right away what we'd done to them. He saw that Kenny had never stopped running and knew that unless the ball beat him to the plate, the game was over. He cut loose his throw in a blink. The whole crowd inhaled at once. Kenny raced the ball.

I told him later that he only slid in for the style points. I said it was my strategy and not his speed that won the game, but that was only half true. Pete Nellis hunkered down to block the plate, but Kenny slid right around him. He was never tagged.

The field filled up with crazy people after that. Even guys in suits and ties who'd stopped by on the way home from work were out there. Everybody was going wild because we'd finally beaten Ryder. Our whole dugout swarmed Kenny in a huge pile just behind the plate.

When he fought his way out he came charging at me. Halfway up the first-base line, we grabbed each other and he spun me around. We tried to go looking for Ratch, but everyone converged on us and we both fell down.

I guess I was on the ground when the spell started to go away.

Sal made us quit fooling around and line up for the traditional handshake. The whole time the spell kept getting weaker and it started to feel like there was a weasel loose in my stomach. I shook those guys' hands and looked into their faces and the weasel kept eating at me.

By the time I shook Mark Ryder's hand my insides were gone and all I could feel was the hole inside.

People were blowing their car horns. Guys were charging around the field screaming. I just felt like I was going to be sick. In the dugout I sank down on the bench with my head between my knees. My glove was near my feet, so I picked it up and stared into it.

The game was over. It was *just* over, but I already missed it. While we were playing I could convince myself that it meant something and get off on the idea that beating them mattered. But now we'd beaten them. We'd beaten the bastards who'd always beaten us, but the only thing we'd won was a baseball game and even that didn't seem to mean what it used to. They were still them and we were still us and nothing that happened on the stupid field could change that. "My brother should be here," I kept thinking. "My brother should be here." That's when I lost it.

Dad was the first one who found me, and it seemed like he knew what I was thinking. I couldn't remember any of the things I meant to say to him, so I just said, "All the hard parts start now."

"The hard part started a long time ago," he said.

"We have to keep beating them and beating them and beating them."

"At least now we know how."

25

The Cowboy's friend sat at our kitchen table all night with my mother and father and me. He took a lot of notes and drank a lot of coffee and fiddled with his tape recorder. All through the interview I kept waiting for Cy Ryder or the police or somebody to come crashing through the back door, but I guess that just happens on cop shows. When he knew everything that we knew and how it was that we'd come to know it, he got ready to leave.

That was almost three weeks ago and we've pretty much developed a new routine in our house now. It feels like we're training for a fight or getting ready for a storm. My father reads the want ads in the morning, works on the plumbing in the afternoon, and writes letters at night. He thinks maybe a major league baseball team might need a scout in our area someday. My mother works extra hours, so I do extra chores. On the weekends they try to put together jigsaw puzzles or visit one of my aunts.

Nothing has come out in the paper yet, but right before he left, the Cowboy told me that these things take time. The reporter said that if he was able to put the whole thing together, he wanted to talk to us again, for another story about how we felt "during this ordeal." It sounded a little like that assignment Mrs. Greendress gave us in social studies, about how we came to live where we live.

I guess it is okay to talk about that stuff now, but I am still not sure what I want to say.

You can go for a long while being poorer than other people or powerless before them, but you don't know it until something happens or somebody lets you in on it. Then you can't tell right away if that person did you a favor or not. I was happier before I knew about these things, but I guess I'm wiser now. I'm still not sure if it is possible to be happy about being wise.

Some good things have happened to me since the accident and sooner or later, I think, some good things will happen to my parents, too. These things wouldn't have happened if Billy didn't die, but given a choice we would never have wanted to know them. Not that you get a choice, you just get to deal with it and I guess God grades you from there.

Three mornings a week I go running with Kenny Bibb. The Blue Jays are 4–2 now, with the toughest part of our schedule behind us. We have an outside shot at making the play-offs.

I feel the closest to my brother when we're playing, but not only for the reasons you might think. He always said that baseball was his way out of this place, so I guess playing it keeps me thinking about what my way out is going to be.

The only person I talk about that with is Annie Dunham. Sometimes we sit at No-Name Park and look down in the valley and imagine what it would be like if we could make it over. "I wouldn't even go away to school if I could make it over," she said once. But she can't, so she will go away, and maybe so will I.

Annie likes movies, but she doesn't mind going to a minor league baseball game every now and then. She loves the symphony, but mostly we go dancing to old-time rock 'n' roll. Sometimes we drive to no place in particular, drink tea, and come back. In the summer we are going to go to New York City and find out what it looks like.

Someday maybe I will tell her what I figured out right before Mark Ryder decked me on that double play. Not yet. When somebody dies you learn that eventually you will lose everybody, or that they will lose you. But you also learn that by finding other people, you can heal yourself.

At least it seems that way to me now. Maybe that's just a matter of timing, or having had the chance to watch Annie Dunham fall asleep. I can't really say. It just seems that the having and losing and having and losing spin out that way through your entire life. It's not such a reassuring thing to think about, I guess. But, at least for a little while, you get to feel quiet at the center of yourself.

213